DOVER · THRIFT · EDITIONS

Coriolanus

WILLIAM SHAKESPEARE

DOVER PUBLICATIONS, INC.
Mineola, New York

DOVER THRIFT EDITIONS

GENERAL EDITOR: PAUL NEGRI
EDITOR OF THIS VOLUME: TOM CRAWFORD

Theatrical Rights

This Dover Thrift Edition may be used in its entirety, in adaptation, or in any other way for theatrical productions, professional and amateur, in the United States, without fee, permission, or acknowledgment. (This may not apply outside of the United States, as copyright conditions may vary.)

Bibliographical Note

This Dover edition, first published in 2003, contains the unabridged text of *Coriolanus*, as published in Volume XIX of *The Caxton Edition of the Complete Works of William Shakespeare*, Caxton Publishing Company, London, n.d. The Note was specially prepared for this edition, and explanatory footnotes from the Caxton edition have been edited.

Library of Congress Cataloging-in-Publication Data

Shakespeare, William, 1564–1616.
 Coriolanus / William Shakespeare.
  p. cm. — (Dover thrift editions)
 ISBN 0-486-42688-2 (pbk.)
  1. Coriolanus, Caius Marcius—Drama. 2. Generals—Drama. 3. Rome—Drama.
I. Title. II. Series.

PR2805.A1 2003
822.3'3—dc21

                      2002041720

Manufactured in the United States of America
Dover Publications, Inc., 31 East 2nd Street, Mineola, N.Y. 11501

Note

CONSIDERED BY T. S. Eliot to be the finest of Shakespeare's tragedies (an opinion not shared by most other critics), *Coriolanus* was directly derived from Sir Thomas North's celebrated translation of Plutarch's *Lives of the Noble Grecians and Romans*. Indeed, Shakespeare followed his model so closely that later commentators have found the Plutarch/North version of immense help in restoring and interpreting lost or obscure passages in the play. Shakespeare, of course, brought his incomparable poetic and dramatic genius to bear in telling the story of the prideful and arrogant Roman general, raising Coriolanus close to the lofty plane of Lear, Macbeth, Hamlet, and other Shakespearean tragic heroes.

Probably written in 1608 or 1609, the play was printed in the First Folio of 1623. The only previously known dramatic treatment of the Coriolanus story was a French play, by Alexandre Hardy, staged in Paris circa 1607. Shakespeare may or may not have been aware of Hardy's work, but in Shakespeare's hands, the tale achieves far greater tragic passion than the French version. Unfortunately, the text of Shakespeare's play that has come down to us is substantially corrupt; a circumstance that has long challenged the abilities of textual critics. Some passages still remain barely intelligible. Nevertheless, the play brings its great protagonist and supporting characters fully to life, suggesting classical Greek drama in its portrayal of Coriolanus' downfall as the result of a fatal character flaw—the sin of hubris or pride.

In addition to the drama of Coriolanus' personal fate, there are also interesting political themes in the play. In the opening scene's famous "belly" speech, Menenius, a patrician senator (and close friend of Coriolanus) likens the state to a body in which the aristocrats are the belly and the lower classes are the "toe." This analogy suggests a source for the enmity between the patricians and the plebeians in Shakespeare's play, centering around the aristocrats' hoarding of corn to the detriment of the commoners. And in reality, there were food riots in England just a year before *Coriolanus* was first performed, sparked by the perception of the poor that the upper classes were hoarding grain. Shakespeare, however, had to handle this theme with some delicacy to avoid antagonizing the aristocrats who were his patrons, and also formed a significant part of his audience.

That audience would also have understood the theme of conflict between filial piety and the political and military obligations of Coriolanus. On the point of conquering Rome at the head of the Volscians, he yields to his mother's passionate pleas for mercy for his family and his erstwhile Roman countrymen. One of the few people able to exercise any sway over her strong-minded son, Volumnia is one of Shakespeare's great female creations, a woman of courage, principle, and nobility. With his act of filial obedience to her, Coriolanus in effect seals his own fate at the hands of the Volscians, bringing an end to his life and career, and closing out this masterly drama.

Contents

Dramatis Personæ   vi

Act I   1

Act II   29

Act III   54

Act IV   78

Act V   101

Dramatis Personæ[1]

CAIUS MARCIUS, afterwards CAIUS MARCIUS CORIOLANUS.
TITUS LARTIUS, ⎫
COMINIUS,   ⎬ generals against the Volscians.
MENENIUS AGRIPPA, friend to Coriolanus.
SICINIUS VELUTUS, ⎫
JUNIUS BRUTUS, ⎬ tribunes of the people.
YOUNG MARCIUS, son of Coriolanus.
A Roman Herald.
TULLUS AUFIDIUS, general of the Volscians.
Lieutenant to Aufidius.
Conspirators with Aufidius.
A Citizen of Antium.
Two Volscian Guards.

VOLUMNIA, mother to Coriolanus.
VIRGILIA, wife to Coriolanus.
VALERIA, friend to Virgilia.
Gentlewoman attending on Virgilia.

Roman and Volscian Senators, Patricians, Ædiles, Lictors, Soldiers,
Citizens, Messengers, Servants to Aufidius, and other Attendants.

SCENE: *Rome and the neighbourhood; Corioli and the neighbourhood;*
Antium

[1]The piece was first printed in the First Folio of 1623.

ACT I.

SCENE I. *Rome. A Street.*

Enter a company of mutinous Citizens, *with staves, clubs, and other weapons*

FIRST CITIZEN.   Before we proceed any further, hear me speak.

ALL.   Speak, speak.

FIRST CIT.   You are all resolved rather to die than to famish?

ALL.   Resolved, resolved.

FIRST CIT.   First, you know Caius Marcius is chief enemy to the people.

ALL.   We know't, we know't.

FIRST CIT.   Let us kill him, and we'll have corn at our own price. Is 't a verdict?

ALL.   No more talking on 't; let it be done: away, away!   10

SEC. CIT.   One word, good citizens.

FIRST CIT.   We are accounted poor citizens; the patricians, good. What authority surfeits on would relieve us: if they would yield us but the superfluity while it were wholesome, we might guess they relieved us humanely; but they think we are too dear: the leanness that afflicts us, the object of our misery, is as an inventory to particularize their abundance; our sufferance is a gain to them. Let us revenge this with our pikes, ere we become rakes: for the gods know I speak this in hunger for bread, not in thirst for revenge.   20

9 *Is 't a verdict?*] Is that our unanimous decision?

13 *good*] in the mercantile sense of substantial, well to do. Cf. *Merch. of Ven.*, I, iii, 12: "Antonio is a *good* man."

15–16 *they think we are too dear*] they think the expense of maintaining us is more than we are worth.

16 *object*] outward aspect, spectacle.

17 *particularize*] describe in detail.

18 *our sufferance . . . to them*] they gain by our suffering. The general sense is that our loss is their gain.

19 *we become rakes*] a reference to the proverbial expression "as lean as a rake."

1

SEC. CIT. Would you proceed especially against Caius Marcius?

ALL. Against him first: he's a very dog to the commonalty.

SEC. CIT. Consider you what services he has done for his country?

FIRST CIT. Very well; and could be content to give him good report for 't, but that he pays himself with being proud.

SEC. CIT. Nay, but speak not maliciously.

FIRST CIT. I say unto you, what he hath done famously, he did it to that end: though soft-conscienced men can be content 30
to say it was for his country, he did it to please his mother and to be partly proud; which he is, even to the altitude of his virtue.

SEC. CIT. What he cannot help in his nature, you account a vice in him. You must in no way say he is covetous.

FIRST CIT. If I must not, I need not be barren of accusations; he hath faults, with surplus, to tire in repetition. [*Shouts within.*] What shouts are these? The other side o' the city is risen: why stay we prating here? to the Capitol!

ALL. Come, come. 40

FIRST CIT. Soft! who comes here?

Enter MENENIUS AGRIPPA

SEC. CIT. Worthy Menenius Agrippa; one that hath always loved the people.

FIRST CIT. He's one honest enough: would all the rest were so!

MEN. What work's, my countrymen, in hand? where go you With bats and clubs? the matter? speak, I pray you.

FIRST CIT. Our business is not unknown to the senate; they have had inkling, this fortnight, what we intend to do, which now we'll show 'em in deeds. They say poor suitors have strong breaths: they shall know we have strong arms too. 50

MEN. Why, masters, my good friends, mine honest neighbours, Will you undo yourselves?

FIRST CIT. We cannot, sir, we are undone already.

MEN. I tell you, friends, most charitable care
Have the patricians of you. For your wants,
Your suffering in this dearth, you may as well
Strike at the heaven with your staves as lift them
Against the Roman state; whose course will on

---

32 *and to be partly proud . . . virtue*] and in part to indulge his pride; he is fully as proud as he is valorous.

The way it takes, cracking ten thousand curbs
Of more strong link asunder than can ever   60
Appear in your impediment. For the dearth,
The gods, not the patricians, make it, and
Your knees to them, not arms, must help. Alack,
You are transported by calamity
Thither where more attends you, and you slander
The helms o' the state, who care for you like fathers,
When you curse them as enemies.

FIRST CIT.   Care for us! True, indeed! They ne'er cared for us
yet: suffer us to famish, and their storehouses crammed with
grain; make edicts for usury, to support usurers; repeal daily   70
any wholesome act established against the rich, and provide
more piercing statutes daily, to chain up and restrain the
poor. If the wars eat us not up, they will; and there's all the
love they bear us.

MEN.   Either you must
Confess yourselves wondrous malicious,
Or be accused of folly. I shall tell you
A pretty tale: it may be you have heard it;
But, since it serves my purpose, I will venture
To stale 't a little more.   80

FIRST CIT.   Well, I'll hear it, sir: yet you must not think to fob off
our disgrace with a tale: but, an 't please you, deliver.

MEN.   There was a time when all the body's members
Rebell'd against the belly; thus accused it:
That only like a gulf it did remain
I' the midst o' the body, idle and unactive,
Still cupboarding the viand, never bearing
Like labour with the rest; where the other instruments
Did see and hear, devise, instruct, walk, feel,
And, mutually participate, did minister   90
Unto the appetite and affection common
Of the whole body. The belly answer'd—

66 *helms*] helmsmen, pilots.
69–70 *suffer us to famish . . . usurers*] Plutarch distinguishes two separate popular out-
     breaks, one on account of the extortion of usurers, and the other on account of
     famine. Shakespeare combines the two.
80 *stale 't*] make it common or familiar. Cf. *Ant and Cleop.*, II, ii, 239–240: "Age can-
     not wither her, nor custom *stale* Her infinite variety."
81–82 *fob off our disgrace*] offer a deceitful excuse for our hardship or injury, delude us
     in our misery. For the alternative form "fubbed off" cf. *2 Hen. IV*, II, i, 32.
88 *where*] whereas.

FIRST CIT.   Well, sir, what answer made the belly?
MEN.   Sir, I shall tell you. With a kind of smile,
　　　Which ne'er came from the lungs, but even thus—
　　　For, look you, I may make the belly smile
　　　As well as speak—it tauntingly replied
　　　To the discontented members, the mutinous parts
　　　That envied his receipt; even so most fitly
　　　As you malign our senators for that　　　　　　　　　100
　　　They are not such as you.
FIRST CIT.　　　　　　　　Your belly's answer? What!
　　　The kingly-crowned head, the vigilant eye,
　　　The counsellor heart, the arm our soldier,
　　　Our steed the leg, the tongue our trumpeter,
　　　With other muniments and petty helps
　　　In this our fabric, if that they—
MEN.　　　　　　　　　　What then?
　　　'Fore me, this fellow speaks! what then? what then?
FIRST CIT.　Should by the cormorant belly be restrain'd,　　110
　　　Who is the sink o' the body,—
MEN.　　　　　　　　　Well, what then?
FIRST CIT.　The former agents, if they did complain,
　　　What could the belly answer?
MEN.　　　　　　　　I will tell you;
　　　If you'll bestow a small—of what you have little—
　　　Patience awhile, you'st hear the belly's answer.
FIRST CIT.　You're long about it.
MEN.　　　　　　　　　Note me this, good friend;
　　　Your most grave belly was deliberate,　　　　　　120
　　　Not rash like his accusers, and thus answer'd:
　　　"True is it, my incorporate friends," quoth he,
　　　"That I receive the general food at first,
　　　Which you do live upon; and fit it is,
　　　Because I am the store-house and the shop
　　　Of the whole body: but, if you do remember,
　　　I send it through the rivers of your blood,

94–95 *a kind of smile . . . lungs*] Hearty laughter was commonly supposed to come di-
　　rect from the lungs. Cf. *As you like it*, II, vii, 30: "My *lungs* began to crow like chan-
　　ticleer."
99 *most fitly*] exactly.
104 *counsellor heart*] The heart was reckoned the seat of the understanding. Cf. line
　　128, *infra*.

Even to the court, the heart, to the seat o' the brain;
And, through the cranks and offices of man,
The strongest nerves and small inferior veins   130
From me receive that natural competency
Whereby they live: and though that all at once,
You, my good friends,"—this says the belly, mark me,—
FIRST CIT.   Ay, sir; well, well.
MEN.   "Though all at once cannot
See what I do deliver out to each,
Yet I can make my audit up, that all
From me do back receive the flour of all,
And leave me but the bran." What say you to 't?
FIRST CIT.   It was an answer: how apply you this?   140
MEN.   The senators of Rome are this good belly,
And you the mutinous members: for examine
Their counsels and their cares, digest things rightly
Touching the weal o' the common, you shall find
No public benefit which you receive
But it proceeds or comes from them to you
And no way from yourselves. What do you think,
You, the great toe of this assembly?
FIRST CIT.   I the great toe! why the great toe?
MEN.   For that, being one o' the lowest, basest, poorest,   150
Of this most wise rebellion, thou go'st foremost:
Thou rascal, that art worst in blood to run,
Lead'st first to win some vantage.
But make you ready your stiff bats and clubs:
Rome and her rats are at the point of battle;
The one side must have bale.

Enter CAIUS MARCIUS

                   Hail, noble Marcius!
MAR.   Thanks. What's the matter, you dissentious rogues,

128 *to the seat o' the brain*] even to the royal residence of the thinking faculty, which, according to the old physiology, was the heart. Cf. line 104, *supra*, and note.
129 *cranks and offices*] winding passages and working-chambers.
130 *nerves*] sinews, muscle.
144 *weal o' the common*] welfare of the common people.
152 *rascal*] The word was specifically applied to a deer in bad condition and unfit for the chase.
152 *in blood to run*] in condition for running.
156 *have bale*] suffer ruin. "Bale" had become an archaic word in Shakespeare's day.

That, rubbing the poor itch of your opinion,
Make yourselves scabs? 160
FIRST CIT. We have ever your good word.
MAR. He that will give good words to thee will flatter
Beneath abhorring. What would you have, you curs,
That like nor peace nor war? the one affrights you,
The other makes you proud. He that trusts to you,
Where he should find you lions, finds you hares,
Where foxes, geese: you are no surer, no,
Than is the coal of fire upon the ice,
Or hailstone in the sun. Your virtue is
To make him worthy whose offence subdues him 170
And curse that justice did it. Who deserves greatness
Deserves your hate; and your affections are
A sick man's appetite, who desires most that
Which would increase his evil. He that depends
Upon your favours swims with fins of lead
And hews down oaks with rushes. Hang ye! Trust ye?
With every minute you do change a mind,
And call him noble that was now your hate,
Him vile that was your garland. What's the matter,
That in these several places of the city 180
You cry against the noble senate, who,
Under the gods, keep you in awe, which else
Would feed on one another? What's their seeking?
MEN. For corn at their own rates; whereof, they say,
The city is well stored.
MAR. Hang 'em! They say!
They'll sit by the fire, and presume to know
What's done i' the Capitol; who's like to rise,
Who thrives and who declines; side factions and give out
Conjectural marriages; making parties strong, 190
And feebling such as stand not in their liking

---

160 *scabs*] a common term of contemptuous reproach.
163 *Beneath abhorring*] What is beneath contempt.
169–171 *Your virtue is . . . did it*] Your notion of virtue is to treat as worthy of honour
   him who is brought low or conquered by crime, and to curse that justice which
   paid him his desserts.
179 *your garland*] your ornament, your crown. Cf. *Ant and Cleop.*, IV, xv, 64: "wither'd
   is *the garland* of the war."
189 *side factions and give out*] (who) take sides in or support factions, and (who) announce.
190 *making parties strong*] strengthening some parties or factions.

Below their cobbled shoes. They say there's grain enough!
Would the nobility lay aside their ruth,
And let me use my sword, I 'ld make a quarry
With thousands of these quarter'd slaves, as high
As I could pick my lance.
MEN.   Nay, these are almost thoroughly persuaded;
For though abundantly they lack discretion,
Yet are they passing cowardly. But, I beseech you,
What says the other troop?   200
MAR.   They are dissolved: hang 'em!
They said they were an-hungry; sigh'd forth proverbs,
That hunger broke stone walls, that dogs must eat,
That meat was made for mouths, that the gods sent not
Corn for the rich men only: with these shreds
They vented their complainings; which being answer'd,
And a petition granted them, a strange one—
To break the heart of generosity
And make bold power look pale—they threw their caps
As they would hang them on the horns o' the moon,   210
Shouting their emulation.
MEN.   What is granted them?
MAR.   Five tribunes to defend their vulgar wisdoms,
Of their own choice: one's Junius Brutus,
Sicinius Velutus, and I know not—'Sdeath!
The rabble should have first unroof'd the city,
Ere so prevail'd with me: it will in time
Win upon power and throw forth greater themes
For insurrection's arguing.
MEN.   This is strange.   220
MAR.   Go get you home, you fragments!

Enter a Messenger, *hastily*

MESS.   Where's Caius Marcius?
MAR.   Here: what's the matter?

193 *their ruth*] their pitying tenderness.
194 *a quarry*] a heap of deer slaughtered in the chase.
195 *quarter'd slaves*] slaves cut down by the sword. Cf. *Jul. Cæs.*, III, i, 268: "Their in-
    fants *quarter'd* with the hands of war."
196 *pick*] pitch.
205 *these shreds*] these odds and ends.
208 *To break the heart of generosity*] To take the heart or life out of the power of nobil-
    ity, to give the power of the nobles its deathblow.
211 *emulation*] envy or factious rivalry.
219 *For insurrection's arguing*] To be discussed by means of insurrection.

MESS.   The news is, sir, the Volsces are in arms.
MAR.   I am glad on 't: then we shall ha' means to vent
    Our musty superfluity. See, our best elders.

Enter COMINIUS, TITUS LARTIUS, *and other* Senators; JUNIUS
    BRUTUS *and* SICINIUS VELUTUS

FIRST SEN.   Marcius, 't is true that you have lately told us;
    The Volsces are in arms.
MAR.   They have a leader,
    Tullus Aufidius, that will put you to 't.   230
    I sin in envying his nobility;
    And were I any thing but what I am,
    I would wish me only he.
COM.   You have fought together?
MAR.   Were half to half the world by the ears, and he
    Upon my party, I'ld revolt, to make
    Only my wars with him: he is a lion
    That I am proud to hunt.
FIRST SEN.   Then, worthy Marcius,
    Attend upon Cominius to these wars.   240
COM.   It is your former promise.
MAR.   Sir, it is;
    And I am constant. Titus Lartius, thou
    Shalt see me once more strike at Tullus' face.
    What, art thou stiff? stand'st out?
TIT.   No, Caius Marcius;
    I'll lean upon one crutch, and fight with t' other,
    Ere stay behind this business.
MEN.   O, true-bred!
FIRST SEN.   Your company to the Capitol; where, I know,   250
    Our greatest friends attend us.
TIT.   [*To* Com.] Lead you on.
    [*To* Mar.] Follow Cominius; we must follow you;
    Right worthy you priority.
COM.   Noble Marcius!
FIRST SEN.   [*To the* Citizens] Hence to your homes; be gone!
MAR.   Nay, let them follow:
    The Volsces have much corn; take these rats thither

225–226 *vent Our musty superfluity*] work off our mouldy superfluity of population.
230 *put you to 't*] put you on your mettle.
236 *Upon my party*] On my side.
245 *art thou stiff?*] are your limbs too stiff to join in fight?

To gnaw their garners. Worshipful mutiners,
Your valour puts well forth: pray, follow.   260

    [Citizens *steal away. Exeunt all but* SICINIUS *and* BRUTUS.

SIC.   Was ever man so proud as is this Marcius?
BRU. He has no equal.
SIC.   When we were chosen tribunes for the people,—
BRU. Mark'd you his lip and eyes?
SIC.   Nay, but his taunts.
BRU. Being moved, he will not spare to gird the gods.
SIC.   Bemock the modest moon.
BRU.   The present wars devour him! he is grown
Too proud to be so valiant.
SIC.   Such a nature,   270
Tickled with good success, disdains the shadow
Which he treads on at noon: but I do wonder
His insolence can brook to be commanded
Under Cominius.
BRU.   Fame, at the which he aims,
In whom already he's well graced, cannot
Better be held, nor more attain'd, than by
A place below the first: for what miscarries
Shall be the general's fault, though he perform
To the utmost of a man; and giddy censure   280
Will then cry out of Marcius "O, if he
Had borne the business!"
SIC.   Besides, if things go well,
Opinion, that so sticks on Marcius, shall
Of his demerits rob Cominius.
BRU.   Come:
Half all Cominius' honours are to Marcius,
Though Marcius earn'd them not; and all his faults
To Marcius shall be honours, though indeed
In aught he merit not.   290

---

259 *Worshipful mutiners . . . forth*] Honoured rebels, your valour looks promising.
266 *gird*] sneer at.
269 *Too proud to be*] Too proud of being.
271 *Tickled with good success*] Pleased, put in a good humour by the good result of his activity.
280 *giddy*] inexperienced, thoughtless.
285 *demerits*] The general repute that Marcius so firmly enjoys shall rob Cominius of his due praise. "Demerits" is constantly used in the sense of "merits."

SIC.   Let 's hence, and hear
        How the dispatch is made; and in what fashion,
        More than his singularity, he goes
        Upon this present action.
BRU.   Let 's along.   [*Exeunt.*

SCENE II. *Corioli. The Senate-House.*

Enter TULLUS AUFIDIUS, *with* Senators *of Corioli*

FIRST SEN.   So, your opinion is, Aufidius,
        That they of Rome are enter'd in our counsels,
        And know how we proceed.
AUF.   Is it not yours?
        What ever have been thought on in this state,
        That could be brought to bodily act ere Rome
        Had circumvention? 'T is not four days gone
        Since I heard thence: these are the words: I think
        I have the letter here: yes, here it is:
        [*Reads*] "They have press'd a power, but it is not known   10
        Whether for east or west: the dearth is great;
        The people mutinous: and it is rumour'd,
        Cominius, Marcius your old enemy,
        Who is of Rome worse hated than of you,
        And Titus Lartius, a most valiant Roman,
        These three lead on this preparation
        Whither 't is bent: most likely 't is for you:
        Consider of it."
FIRST SEN.   Our army 's in the field:
        We never yet made doubt but Rome was ready   20
        To answer us.
AUF.   Nor did you think it folly
        To keep your great pretences veil'd till when
        They needs must show themselves; which in the hatching,
        It seem'd, appear'd to Rome. By the discovery

---

293 *More than his singularity*] Apart from the (haughty manner that is) characteristic of
    his individuality.

---

  2 *are enter'd in our counsels*] have gained entry into or knowledge of our counsels.
  7 *Had circumvention*] Had got the knowledge wherewith to circumvent or outwit our
    plans.
10 *press'd a power*] impressed or enlisted troops by force.
16 *preparation*] army ready for the field.
23 *great pretences*] important intentions.

We shall be shorten'd in our aim, which was
To take in many towns ere almost Rome
Should know we were afoot.
SEC. SEN.   Noble Aufidius,
Take your commission; hie you to your bands: 30
Let us alone to guard Corioli:
If they set down before 's, for the remove
Bring up your army; but, I think, you'll find
They've not prepared for us.
AUF.   O, doubt not that;
I speak from certainties. Nay, more,
Some parcels of their power are forth already,
And only hitherward. I leave your honours.
If we and Caius Marcius chance to meet,
'T is sworn between us, we shall ever strike   40
Till one can do no more.
ALL.   The gods assist you!
AUF.   And keep your honours safe!
FIRST SEN.   Farewell.
SEC. SEN.   Farewell.
ALL.   Farewell.   [*Exeunt.*

SCENE III. *Rome. A Room in Marcius' House.*

Enter VOLUMNIA *and* VIRGILIA: *they set them down on two low
stools, and sew*

VOL.   I pray you, daughter, sing, or express yourself in a more
comfortable sort: if my son were my husband, I should free-
lier rejoice in that absence wherein he won honour than in
the embracements of his bed where he would show most
love. When yet he was but tender-bodied, and the only son
of my womb; when youth with comeliness plucked all gaze
his way; when, for a day of kings' entreaties, a mother should
not sell him an hour from her beholding; I, considering how

---

26 *shorten'd in our aim*] hindered in our project.
27 *take in*] conquer, subdue: a common usage. Cf. III, ii, 73, *infra*.
32–33 *If they . . . your army*] If the Romans sit down before (*i.e.*, besiege) us, bring up
     the army in order to remove or dislodge them.
40 *we shall ever strike*] we shall keep on attacking one another.

---

2 *comfortable*] cheerful.
6–7 *when youth . . . his way*] when his youthful beauty attracted every one's attention.

honour would become such a person; that it was no better
than picture-like to hang by the wall, if renown made it not   10
stir, was pleased to let him seek danger where he was like to
find fame. To a cruel war I sent him; from whence he re-
turned, his brows bound with oak. I tell thee, daughter, I
sprang not more in joy at first hearing he was a man-child
than now in first seeing he had proved himself a man.

VIR.   But had he died in the business, madam: how then?

VOL.   Then his good report should have been my son; I therein
would have found issue. Hear me profess sincerely: had I a
dozen sons, each in my love alike, and none less dear than
thine and my good Marcius, I had rather had eleven die   20
nobly for their country than one voluptuously surfeit out of
action.

Enter a Gentlewoman

GENT.   Madam, the Lady Valeria is come to visit you.

VIR.   Beseech you, give me leave to retire myself.

VOL.   Indeed, you shall not.
    Methinks I hear hither your husband's drum;
    See him pluck Aufidius down by the hair;
    As children from a bear, the Volsces shunning him:
    Methinks I see him stamp thus, and call thus:
    "Come on, you cowards! you were got in fear,   30
    Though you were born in Rome:" his bloody brow
    With his mail'd hand then wiping, forth he goes,
    Like to a harvest-man that 's task'd to mow
    Or all, or lose his hire.

VIR.   His bloody brow! O Jupiter, no blood!

VOL.   Away, you fool! it more becomes a man
    Than gilt his trophy: the breasts of Hecuba,
    When she did suckle Hector, look'd not lovelier
    Than Hector's forehead when it spit forth blood
    At Grecian sword, contemning. Tell Valeria   40
    We are fit to bid her welcome.   [*Exit* Gent.

---

13 *his brows bound with oak*] a crown of oak leaves was awarded to any soldier who saved
    a companion's life in battle.

24 *retire myself*] withdraw.

30 *got*] begotten.

37 *Than gilt his trophy*] Than gold or gilding becomes the decorated monument or
    memorial set up in honour of a general's victory.

40 *At Grecian sword, contemning*] Thus Collier; "contemning" being treated as a par-
    ticiple used adverbially, *i.e.*, "contemptuously."

VIR.   Heavens bless my lord from fell Aufidius!
VOL.   He'll beat Aufidius' head below his knee,
       And tread upon his neck.

Enter VALERIA, *with an* Usher *and* Gentlewoman

VAL.   My ladies both, good day to you.
VOL.   Sweet madam.
VIR.   I am glad to see your ladyship.
VAL.   How do you both? you are manifest housekeepers. What
       are you sewing here? A fine spot, in good faith. How does
       your little son?   50
VIR.   I thank your ladyship; well, good madam.
VOL.   He had rather see the swords and hear a drum than look
       upon his schoolmaster.
VAL.   O' my word, the father's son: I'll swear, 't is a very pretty
       boy. O' my troth, I looked upon him o' Wednesday half an
       hour together; has such a confirmed countenance. I saw
       him run after a gilded butterfly; and when he caught it, he
       let it go again; and after it again; and over and over he
       comes, and up again; catched it again: or whether his fall en-
       raged him, or how 't was, he did so set his teeth, and tear it; 60
       O, I warrant, how he mammocked it!
VOL.   One on 's father's moods.
VAL.   Indeed, la 't is a noble child.
VIR.   A crack, madam.
VAL.   Come, lay aside your stitchery; I must have you play the
       idle huswife with me this afternoon.
VIR.   No, good madam; I will not out of doors.
VAL.   Not out of doors!
VOL.   She shall, she shall.
VIR.   Indeed, no, by your patience; I'll not over the threshold till 70
       my lord return from the wars.
VAL.   Fie, you confine yourself most unreasonably: come, you
       must go visit the good lady that lies in.

---

48 *manifest housekeepers*] evident stay-at-homes.
49 A *fine spot*] A small or delicate pattern in the embroidery.
56 *confirmed countenance*] steady, firm look. Cf. *Much Ado*, V, iv, 17: "Which I will do
    with *confirm'd countenance."*
61 *mammocked*] tore in pieces. "Mammock" is often found in the sense of morsel or
    fragment.
62 *moods*] fits of passion.
64 A *crack*] A sprightly precocious lad.

VIR.   I will wish her speedy strength, and visit her with my prayers; but I cannot go thither.

VOL.   Why, I pray you?

VIR.   'T is not to save labour, nor that I want love.

VAL.   You would be another Penelope: yet, they say, all the yarn she spun in Ulysses' absence did but fill Ithaca full of moths. Come; I would your cambric were sensible as your finger,   80 that you might leave pricking it for pity. Come, you shall go with us.

VIR.   No, good madam, pardon me; indeed, I will not forth.

VAL.   In truth, la, go with me, and I'll tell you excellent news of your husband.

VIR.   O, good madam, there can be none yet.

VAL.   Verily, I do not jest with you; there came news from him last night.

VIR.   Indeed, madam?

VAL.   In earnest, it's true; I heard a senator speak it. Thus it is: 90 the Volsces have an army forth; against whom Cominius the general is gone, with one part of our Roman power: your lord and Titus Lartius are set down before their city Corioli; they nothing doubt prevailing, and to make it brief wars. This is true, on mine honour; and so, I pray, go with us.

VIR.   Give me excuse, good madam; I will obey you in every thing hereafter.

VOL.   Let her alone, lady; as she is now, she will but disease our better mirth.

VAL.   In troth, I think she would. Fare you well, then. Come,   100 good sweet lady. Prithee, Virgilia, turn thy solemness out o' door, and go along with us.

VIR.   No, at a word, madam; indeed, I must not. I wish you much mirth.

VAL.   Well then, farewell.   [*Exeunt.*

---

80 *sensible*] sensitive, susceptible of feeling.

94 *they nothing . . . brief wars*] they have no sort of doubt of their victory and of making the war a brief one.

98 *disease*] spoil.

103 *at a word*] in short, once for all.

Scene IV. *Before Corioli.*

Enter, with drum and colours, Marcius, Titus Lartius,
    Captains *and* Soldiers. *To them a* Messenger

Mar. Yonder comes news: a wager they have met.
Lart. My horse to yours, no.
Mar.   'T is done.
Lart.   Agreed.
Mar. Say, has our general met the enemy?
Mess.   They lie in view; but have not spoke as yet.
Lart. So, the good horse is mine.
Mar.   I'll buy him of you.
Lart. No, I'll nor sell nor give him: lend you him I will
    For half a hundred years. Summon the town.   10
Mar. How far off lie these armies?
Mess.   Within this mile and half.
Mar.   Then shall we hear their 'larum, and they ours.
    Now, Mars, I prithee, make us quick in work,
    That we with smoking swords may march from hence,
    To help our fielded friends! Come, blow thy blast.

They sound a parley. Enter two Senators *with others, on the walls.*

    Tullus Aufidius, is he within your walls?
First Sen.   No, nor a man that fears you less than he,
    That's lesser than a little. Hark, our drums   [*Drum afar off.*
    Are bringing forth our youth! we'll break our walls,   20
    Rather than they shall pound us up: our gates,
    Which yet seem shut, we have but pinn'd with rushes;
    They'll open of themselves. Hark you, far off!
                                                   [*Alarum far off.*
    There is Aufidius; list, what work he makes
    Amongst your cloven army.
Mar.   O, they are at it!
Lart.   Their noise be our instruction. Ladders, ho!

Enter the army of the Volsces

    6 *spoke*] given the signal to engage.
    16 *our fielded friends*] our friends encamped on the field of battle.
    18 *less than he*] there is a tangle here; "less than" has the effect of "more than." The
        meiosis is due to the common practice of employing the double negative to empha-
        sise a negative intention.
    21 *pound us up*] imprison us, bottle us up.

MAR.   They fear us not, but issue forth their city.
   Now put your shields before your hearts, and fight
   With hearts more proof than shields. Advance, brave Titus: 30
   They do disdain us much beyond our thoughts,
   Which makes me sweat with wrath. Come on, my fellows:
   He that retires, I'll take him for a Volsce,
   And he shall feel mine edge.

Alarum. The Romans *are beat back to their trenches. Re-enter*
   MARCIUS, *cursing*

MAR.   All the contagion of the south light on you,
   You shames of Rome! you herd of— Boils and plagues
   Plaster you o'er; that you may be abhorr'd
   Farther than seen, and one infect another
   Against the wind a mile! You souls of geese,
   That bear the shapes of men, how have you run   40
   From slaves that apes would beat! Pluto and hell!
   All hurt behind; backs red, and faces pale
   With flight and agued fear! Mend, and charge home,
   Or, by the fires of heaven, I'll leave the foe,
   And make my wars on you: look to 't: come on;
   If you'll stand fast, we'll beat them to their wives,
   As they us to our trenches followed.

Another alarum. The Volsces *fly, and* MARCIUS *follows them to*
   the gates

   So, now the gates are ope: now prove good seconds
   'T is for the followers fortune widens them,
   Not for the fliers: mark me, and do the like.   50
                              [Enters the gates.

FIRST SOL.   Fool-hardiness; not I.
SEC. SOL.   Nor I.   *[*MARCIUS *is shut in.*
FIRST SOL.   See, they have shut him in.

---

30 *more proof*] more tried, better tested, stouter.
35 *the south*] the south wind which was supposed to bring pestilence in its train. Cf.
   Cymb., II, iii, 131: "The *south*-fog rot him."
36 *you herd of—*] Johnson inserted the dash. Marcius' fury does not permit him to end
   the sentence coherently.
43 *agued fear*] trembling fear; trembling being a main characteristic of an ague fit.
43 *Mend*] correct your errors.
44 *the fires of heaven*] apparently, the stars. "Fires of hell" would seem to be more ap-
   propriate to the context.

ALL.   To the pot, I warrant him.
                          [*Alarum continues.*

Re-enter TITUS LARTIUS

LART.   What is become of Marcius?
ALL.   Slain, sir, doubtless.
FIRST SOL.   Following the fliers at the very heels,
     With them he enters; who, upon the sudden,
     Clapp'd to their gates: he is himself alone,
     To answer all the city.   60
LART.   O noble fellow!
     Who sensibly outdares his senseless sword,
     And, when it bows, stands up! Thou art left, Marcius:
     A carbuncle entire, as big as thou art,
     Were not so rich a jewel. Thou wast a soldier
     Even to Cato's wish, not fierce and terrible
     Only in strokes; but, with thy grim looks and
     The thunder-like percussion of thy sounds,
     Thou madest thine enemies shake, as if the world
     Were feverous and did tremble.   70

Re-enter MARCIUS, *bleeding, assaulted by the enemy*

FIRST SOL.   Look, sir.
LART.   O, 't is Marcius!
     Let 's fetch him off, or make remain alike.
                [*They fight, and all enter the city.*

SCENE V. *Within Corioli. A Street.*

Enter certain Romans, *with spoils*

FIRST ROM.   This will I carry to Rome.
SEC. ROM.   And I this.
THIRD ROM.   A murrain on 't! I took this for silver.
               [*Alarum continues still afar off.*

54 *To the pot*] To ruin; still commonly employed in the vulgarism "gone to pot."
62 *sensibly*] consciously, with full consciousness of his peril.
65 *Thou wast a soldier . . . Cato's wish*] Marcus Porcius Cato, the elder, called "the censor," the great Roman soldier and moralist, who distinguished himself in the second Punic war.
73 *Let's fetch . . . alike*] Let us rescue him, or make our stay here with him.

Enter MARCIUS *and* TITUS LARTIUS *with a trumpet*

MAR.　　See here these movers that do prize their hours
　　　　At a crack'd drachma! Cushions, leaden spoons,
　　　　Irons of a doit, doublets that hangmen would
　　　　Bury with those that wore them, these base slaves,
　　　　Ere yet the fight be done, pack up: down with them!
　　　　And hark, what noise the general makes! To him!
　　　　There is the man of my soul's hate, Aufidius,　　　　　　10
　　　　Piercing our Romans: then, valiant Titus, take
　　　　Convenient numbers to make good the city;
　　　　Whilst I, with those that have the spirit, will haste
　　　　To help Cominius.
LART.　　　　　　　　　　Worthy sir, thou bleed'st;
　　　　Thy exercise hath been too violent
　　　　For a second course of fight.
MAR.　　　　　　　　　　　　Sir, praise me not;
　　　　My work hath yet not warm'd me: fare you well:
　　　　The blood I drop is rather physical　　　　　　　　　　20
　　　　Than dangerous to me: to Aufidius thus
　　　　I will appear, and fight.
LART.　　　　　　　　　　Now the fair goddess, Fortune,
　　　　Fall deep in love with thee; and her great charms
　　　　Misguide thy opposers' swords! Bold gentleman,
　　　　Prosperity be thy page!
MAR.　　　　　　　　　　Thy friend no less
　　　　Than those she placeth highest! So farewell.
LART.　　Thou worthiest Marcius!　　　　　　　　[*Exit* MARCIUS.
　　　　Go sound thy trumpet in the market-place;　　　　　　30
　　　　Call thither all the officers o' the town,
　　　　Where they shall know our mind. Away!　　　　　[*Exeunt.*

---

3 *a trumpet*] a trumpeter. (stage direction)
4 *movers*] probably "stragglers," "loafers." In Plutarch Coriolanus complains at this
　　point of the battle that his men "run straggling here and there."
4 *hours*] time. Thus the Folios. Rowe needlessly substituted *honours.*
5 *drachma*] the Greek coin, which would be unfamiliar at Rome. But Plutarch invari-
　　ably reckons money in Greek currency.
6 *Irons of a doit*] Iron implements worth a doit, *i.e.*, the smallest copper coin.
17 *course of fight*] bout; "course" was technically used of a bout in bear-baiting. Cf.
　　Lear, III, vii, 53: "I am tied to the stake, and I must stand *the course.*"
20 *physical*] wholesome, medicinal.
26 *be thy page*] attend thee, follow thee, as a page boy.

SCENE VI. *Near the Camp of Cominius.*

Enter COMINIUS, *as it were in retire, with* Soldiers

COM.   Breathe you, my friends: well fought; we are come off
        Like Romans, neither foolish in our stands,
        Nor cowardly in retire: believe me, sirs,
        We shall be charged again. Whiles we have struck,
        By interims and conveying gusts we have heard
        The charges of our friends. Ye Roman gods,
        Lead their successes as we wish our own,
        That both our powers, with smiling fronts encountering,
        May give you thankful sacrifice!

Enter a Messenger

                            Thy news?   10
MESS.   The citizens of Corioli have issued,
        And given to Lartius and to Marcius battle:
        I saw our party to their trenches driven,
        And then I came away.
COM.   Though thou speak'st truth,
        Methinks thou speak'st not well. How long is't since?
MESS.   Above an hour, my lord.
COM.   'T is not a mile; briefly we heard their drums:
        How couldst thou in a mile confound an hour,
        And bring thy news so late?   20
MESS.   Spies of the Volsces
        Held me in chase, that I was forced to wheel
        Three or four miles about; else had I, sir,
        Half an hour since brought my report.

Enter MARCIUS

COM.   Who 's yonder,
        That does appear as he were flay'd? O gods!
        He has the stamp of Marcius; and I have
        Before-time seen him thus.

1–3 *we are come off . . . retire*] we have broken off the engagement like Romans, nei-
    ther foolishly making hopeless resistance nor beating a retreat in cowardly wise.
5 *By interims and conveying gusts*] At intervals and by gusts of wind bringing the noise.
11 *issued*] issued forth in a sortie.
18 *briefly*] a short time ago.
19 *confound*] waste or spend. Cf. *1 Hen. IV*, I, iii, 100: "He did *confound* the best part
    of *an hour.*"

MAR.   Come I too late?

COM.   The shepherd knows not thunder from a tabor   30
    More than I know the sound of Marcius' tongue
    From every meaner man.

MAR.   Come I too late?

COM.   Ay, if you come not in the blood of others,
    But mantled in your own.

MAR.   O, let me clip ye
    In arms as sound as when I woo'd; in heart
    As merry as when our nuptial day was done,
    And tapers burn'd to bedward!

COM.   Flower of warriors,   40
    How is't with Titus Lartius?

MAR.   As with a man busied about decrees:
    Condemning some to death, and some to exile;
    Ransoming him or pitying, threatening the other;
    Holding Corioli in the name of Rome,
    Even like a fawning greyhound in the leash,
    To let him slip at will.

COM.   Where is that slave
    Which told me they had beat you to your trenches?
    Where is he? call him hither.   50

MAR.   Let him alone;
    He did inform the truth: but for our gentlemen,
    The common file—a plague! tribunes for them!—
    The mouse ne'er shunn'd the cat as they did budge
    From rascals worse than they.

COM.   But how prevail'd you?

MAR.   Will the time serve to tell? I do not think.
    Where is the enemy? are you lords o' the field?
    If not, why cease you till you are so?

COM.   Marcius,   60
    We have at disadvantage fought, and did
    Retire to win our purpose.

MAR.   How lies their battle? know you on which side
    They have placed their men of trust?

COM.   As I guess, Marcius,

---

30 *tabor*] kettledrum.
44 *Ransoming him or pitying*] Taking ransom of one or setting him free out of pity.
53 *The common file*] The rank and file.
54 *budge*] move away, retreat.
63 *battle*] army arrayed for battle.

Their bands i' the vaward are the Antiates,
Of their best trust; o'er them Aufidius,
Their very heart of hope.
MAR.   I do beseech you,
By all the battles wherein we have fought,   70
By the blood we have shed together, by the vows
We have made to endure friends, that you directly
Set me against Aufidius and his Antiates;
And that you not delay the present, but,
Filling the air with swords advanced and darts,
We prove this very hour.
COM.   Though I could wish
You were conducted to a gentle bath,
And balms applied to you, yet dare I never
Deny your asking: take your choice of those   80
That best can aid your action.
MAR.   Those are they
That most are willing. If any such be here—
As it were sin to doubt—that love this painting
Wherein you see me smear'd; if any fear
Lesser his person than an ill report;
If any think brave death outweighs bad life,
And that his country's dearer than himself;
Let him alone, or so many so minded,
Wave thus, to express his disposition,   90
And follow Marcius.

                    [*They all shout, and wave their swords;*
            take him up in their arms, and cast up their caps.

O, me alone! make you a sword of me?
If these shows be not outward, which of you

---

66 *the Antiates*] Pope's correction of the Folio reading *the Antients*. Plutarch's words
    render the change irrefutable: "The bandes which were *in the vaward* [*i.e.*, the van-
    guard] *of their battell were those of the Antiates* whom they esteemed to be the war-
    likest men," etc. See also line 73, *infra*.

75 *advanced*] upraised.

85–86 *if any fear Lesser . . . report*] if any man cherish less fear on account of his personal
    safety than on account of a bad reputation, if any man set his character above his
    safety. "Lesser," which is read by the Third and Fourth Folios, is not uncommonly
    used for "less." The First and Second Folios read *Lessen*, which makes no sense.

92 *O, me alone! . . . me?*] Thus substantially the Folios, though Capell first inserted the
    note of interrogation at the end of the line. Marcius is rebuking the soldiers for tak-
    ing him up all alone in their arms when he had just bidden them wave or brandish
    their swords. He reproaches his men with making a sword of him.

But is four Volsces? none of you but is
Able to bear against the great Aufidius
A shield as hard as his. A certain number,
Though thanks to all, must I select from all: the rest
Shall bear the business in some other fight,
As cause will be obey'd. Please you to march;
And four shall quickly draw out my command,   100
Which men are best inclined.
COM.   March on, my fellows:
Make good this ostentation, and you shall
Divide in all with us.   [*Exeunt.*

SCENE VII. *The Gates of Corioli.*

TITUS LARTIUS, *having set a guard upon* CORIOLI, *going with
    drum and trumpet toward* COMINIUS *and* CAIUS MARCIUS,
    enters with a Lieutenant, *other* Soldiers, *and a* Scout

LARD.   So, let the ports be guarded: keep your duties,
As I have set them down. If I do send, dispatch   .
Those centuries to our aid; the rest will serve
For a short holding: if we lose the field,
We cannot keep the town.
LIEU.   Fear not our care, sir.
LART.   Hence, and shut your gates upon 's.
Our guider, come; to the Roman camp conduct us.
                                         [*Exeunt.*

SCENE VIII. A *Field of Battle Between the Roman
and the Volscian Camps.*

Alarum as in battle. Enter, from opposite sides, MARCIUS *and*
    AUFIDIUS

MAR.   I'll fight with none but thee; for I do hate thee
Worse than a promise-breaker.

---

99 *As cause will be obey'd*] As occasion shall require.
100–101 *four . . . inclined*] four officers shall quickly select for my command men who
    seem best fitted for the enterprise.
103 *ostentation*] show of courage. "Ostentation" has no ironical shade of meaning here.

---

1 *ports*] gates; so V, vi, 6, *infra.*
3 *centuries*] companies of a hundred men each.

AUF.   We hate alike:
    Not Afric owns a serpent I abhor
    More than thy fame and envy. Fix thy foot.
MAR.   Let the first budger die the other's slave,
    And the gods doom him after!
AUF.   If I fly, Marcius,
    Holloa me like a hare.
MAR.   Within these there hours, Tullus,   10
    Alone I fought in your Corioli walls,
    And made what work I pleased: 't is not my blood
    Wherein thou seest me mask'd; for thy revenge
    Wrench up thy power to the highest.
AUF.   Wert thou the Hector
    That was the whip of your bragg'd progeny,
    Thou shouldst not 'scape me here.

    [*They fight, and certain* Volsces *come in the aid of* AUFIDIUS.
        MARCIUS *fights till they be driven in breathless.*

    Officious, and not valiant, you have shamed me
    In your condemned seconds.   [*Exeunt.*

SCENE IX. *The Roman Camp.*

Flourish. Alarum. A retreat is sounded. Enter, from one side,
COMINIUS *with the* Romans; *from the other side,* MARCIUS,
with his arm in a scarf

COM.   If I should tell thee o'er this thy day's work,
    Thou'lt not believe thy deeds: but I'll report it,
    Where senators shall mingle tears with smiles;
    Where great patricians shall attend, and shrug,
    I' the end admire; where ladies shall be frighted,
    And, gladly quaked, hear more; where the dull tribunes,
    That, with the fusty plebeians, hate thine honours,

---

5 *thy fame and envy*] thy envied fame.
7 *doom him after*] condemn him afterwards.
14 *Wrench up*] Screw up. Cf. *Macb.*, I, vii, 60: "But *screw* your courage to the sticking-place."
16 *the whip . . . progeny*] the scourging champion of your boasted race. The Romans
    claimed descent from the Trojans. Hector was the most valiant of the Trojan chiefs.
18–19 *you have shamed . . . seconds*] you have shamed me by coming to my aid as
    damnable seconds.

---

6 *gladly quaked*] rejoicing in their trembling fears.
7 *plebeians*] usually as here accented by Shakespeare on the first syllable.

Shall say against their hearts "We thank the gods
Our Rome hath such a soldier."
Yet camest thou to a morsel of this feast,   10
Having fully dined before.

Enter TITUS LARTIUS, *with his power, from the pursuit*

LART.   O general,
Here is the steed, we the caparison:
Hadst thou beheld—
MAR.   Pray now, no more: my mother,
Who has a charter to extol her blood,
When she does praise me grieves me. I have done
As you have done; that's what I can: induced
As you have been; that's for my country:
He that has but effected his good will   20
Hath overta'en mine act.
COM.   You shall not be
The grave of your deserving; Rome must know
The value of her own: 't were a concealment
Worse than a theft, no less than a traducement,
To hide your doings; and to silence that,
Which, to the spire and top of praises vouch'd,
Would seem but modest: therefore, I beseech you—
In sign of what you are, not to reward
What you have done—before our army hear me.   30
MAR.   I have some wounds upon me, and they smart
To hear themselves remember'd.
COM.   Should they not,
Well might they fester 'gainst ingratitude,

---

8 *against their-hearts*] unwillingly, in spite of themselves.
10–11 *Yet camest thou . . . before*] This exploit of yours was but a morsel of this feast of
   war, seeing that you had had already a full meal of fighting at Corioli.
13 *Here is the steed . . . caparison*] Here is the man who performed the action. We were
   mere passive ornament of the show.
16 *a charter . . . blood*] a special right or privilege to praise her son.
20–21 *He that . . . act*] He that has merely put into effect his good purpose has outdone
   my own deeds.
23 *The grave of*] That which buries, keeps out of sight.
25 *a traducement*] an act of slander.
26–28 *to silence . . . but modest*] to pass over in silence that which, even when praised
   to the highest pitch, would still suffer from the modesty of the encomium; no praise
   could do full justice to your valour.
33 *Should they not*] sc. be remembered.

And tent themselves with death. Of all the horses,
Whereof we have ta'en good, and good store, of all
The treasure in this field achieved and city,
We render you the tenth; to be ta'en forth,
Before the common distribution, at
Your only choice.   40
MAR.   I thank you, general;
But cannot make my heart consent to take
A bribe to pay my sword: I do refuse it,
And stand upon my common part with those
That have beheld the doing.

    [A *long flourish. They all cry* "Marcius! Marcius!" *cast up their
        caps and lances:* COMINIUS *and* LARTIUS *stand bare.*

MAR.   May these same instruments, which you profane,
Never sound more! when drums and trumpets shall
I' the field prove flatterers, let courts and cities be
Made all of false-faced soothing!
When steel grows soft as the parasite's silk,   50
Let him be made a coverture for the wars!
No more, I say! For that I have not wash'd
My nose that bled, or foil'd some debile wretch,
Which without note here's many else have done,
You shout me forth
In acclamations hyperbolical;
As if I loved my little should be dieted
In praises sauced with lies.

---

35 *tent themselves with death*] find cure in death. "To tent" means literally "to probe
   with a surgical instrument," and hence "to treat surgically," "to dress," "to doctor."
36 *good, and good store*] a good store of excellent qualities.
45 *bare*] bareheaded. (stage direction)
46–51 *May these same instruments . . . coverture for the wars*] Coriolanus is deprecating
   the profanation of the warlike drums and trumpets by making them sound accom-
   paniments to speeches of flattery and compliment. If these instruments of war take
   to playing the part of flatterers in the field of battle, we may very well expect courts
   and cities to be altogether given over to insincere and delusive flattery. When steel
   grows soft as the silk worn by the parasitic courtier, then his thin and flexible garment may serve for the uniform of war. The antecedent of "him" in line 51 seems
   to be "the parasite's silk," and the masculine gender is accounted for by the associa-
   tion of "parasite." *Coverture* is Steevens' substitution for the Folio reading *overture*,
   which might possibly mean the "prelude" or "preparation," and hence "protective
   equipment." But that sense is manifestly strained.
53 *or foil'd some debile wretch*] or because I have vanquished some feeble wretch.
55 *You shout me forth*] You attend me with shouts.

Com.   Too modest are you;
    More cruel to your good report than grateful   60
    To us that give you truly: by your patience,
    If 'gainst yourself you be incensed, we'll put you,
    Like one that means his proper harm, in manacles,
    Then reason safely with you. Therefore, be it known,
    As to us, to all the world, that Caius Marcius
    Wears this war's garland: in token of the which,
    My noble steed, known to the camp, I give him,
    With all his trim belonging; and from this time,
    For what he did before Corioli, call him,
    With all the applause and clamour of the host,   70
    CAIUS MARCIUS CORIOLANUS. Bear
    The addition nobly ever!

                    [*Flourish. Trumpets sound, and drums.*

ALL.   Caius Marcius Coriolanus!
COR.   I will go wash;
    And when my face is fair, you shall perceive
    Whether I blush, or no: howbeit, I thank you:
    I mean to stride your steed; and at all times
    To undercrest your good addition
    To the fairness of my power.
COM.   So, to our tent;   80
    Where, ere we do repose us, we will write
    To Rome of our success. You, Titus Lartius,
    Must to Corioli back: send us to Rome
    The best, with whom we may articulate
    For their own good and ours.
LART.   I shall, my lord.
COR.   The gods begin to mock me. I, that now
    Refused most princely gifts, am bound to beg
    Of my lord general.
COM.   Take't ; 't is yours. What is't?   90
COR.   I sometime lay here in Corioli
    At a poor man's house; he used me kindly:
    He cried to me; I saw him prisoner;

63 *his proper harm*] his own harm, harm to his own person.
78–79 *To undercrest . . . power*] To wear or sustain as a crest or badge of merit the hon-
    ourable title you have bestowed on me, to the best of my ability.
84 *The best . . . articulate*] The best men of Corioli, with whom we may negotiate arti-
    cles of peace.
91–93 *I sometime . . . prisoner*] This incident is drawn almost verbatim from Plutarch.

But then Aufidius was within my view,
And wrath o'erwhelm'd my pity: I request you
To give my poor host freedom.
COM.   O, well begg'd!
Were he the butcher of my son, he should
Be free as is the wind. Deliver him, Titus.
LART.   Marcius, his name?   100
COR.   By Jupiter, forgot:
I am weary; yea, my memory is tired.
Have we no wine here?
COM.   Go we to our tent:
The blood upon your visage dries; 't is time
It should be look'd to: come.   [*Exeunt.*

SCENE X. *The Camp of the Volsces.*

A *flourish. Cornets. Enter* TULLUS AUFIDIUS, *bloody,*
   with two or three Soldiers

AUF.   The town is ta'en!
FIRST SOL.   'T will be deliver'd back on good condition.
AUF.   Condition!
I would I were a Roman; for I cannot,
Being a Volsce, be that I am. Condition!
What good condition can a treaty find
I' the part that is at mercy? Five times, Marcius,
I have fought with thee; so often hast thou beat me;
And wouldst do so, I think, should we encounter
As often as we eat. By the elements,   10
If e'er again I meet him beard to beard,
He's mine, or I am his: mine emulation
Hath not that honour in 't it had; for where
I thought to crush him in an equal force,
True sword to sword, I'll potch at him some way,
Or wrath or craft may get him.
FIRST SOL.   He's the devil.

2 *on good condition*] on favourable terms.
5 *be that I am*] be all that I have a mind to be; or, do that which I feel impelled to do.
12 *mine emulation*] my envy or rivalry. Cf. I, viii, 5, *supra*, where Aufidius says he ab-
   hors Coriolanus' "fame and envy."
13 *where*] whereas.
15 *potch*] thrust, push violently.

AUF.   Bolder, though not so subtle. My valour's poison'd
    With only suffering stain by him; for him
    Shall fly out of itself: nor sleep nor sanctuary,   20
    Being naked, sick, nor fane nor Capitol,
    The prayers of priests nor times of sacrifice,
    Embarquements all of fury, shall lift up
    Their rotten privilege and custom 'gainst
    My hate to Marcius: where I find him, were it
    At home, upon my brother's guard, even there,
    Against the hospitable canon, would I
    Wash my fierce hand in 's heart. Go you to the city;
    Learn how 't is held, and what they are that must
    Be hostages for Rome.   30
FIRST SOL.   Will not you go?
AUF.   I am attended at the cypress grove: I pray you—
    'T is south the city mills—bring me word thither
    How the world goes, that to the pace of it
    I may spur on my journey.
FIRST SOL.   I shall, sir.   [*Exeunt.*

18–20 *My valour's poison'd . . . of itself*] The general sense is that Aufidius' degradation
    at Coriolanus' hands has the effect of converting Aufidius into a cowardly assassin.
    His valour, he says, is poisoned by merely suffering eclipse at his rival's hands, and
    in order to injure his rival, his valour will take leave of its honourable quality.
21 *Being naked, sick*] Did I find Coriolanus naked and ill.
23 *Embarquements all of fury*] embargoes on or impediments to passionate act.
26 *upon my brother's guard*] under my brother's protection.
27 *the hospitable canon*] the law of hospitality.
32 *attended*] waited for. Cf. II, ii, 180, *infra*.

ACT II.

SCENE I. *Rome. A Public Place.*

Enter MENENIUS, *with the two* Tribunes *of the people,* SICINIUS
and BRUTUS

MENENIUS.   The Augurer tells me we shall have news to-night.
BRU.   Good or bad?
MEN.   Not according to the prayer of the people, for they love
  not Marcius.
SIC.   Nature teaches beasts to know their friends.
MEN.   Pray you, who does the wolf love?
SIC.   The lamb.
MEN.   Ay, to devour him; as the hungry plebeians would the
  noble Marcius.
BRU.   He 's a lamb indeed, that baes like a bear.   10
MEN.   He's a bear indeed, that lives like a lamb. You two are old
  men: tell me one thing that I shall ask you.
BOTH.   Well, sir.
MEN.   In what enormity is Marcius poor in, that you two have
  not in abundance?
BRU.   He's poor in no one fault, but stored with all.
SIC.   Especially in pride.
BRU.   And topping all others in boasting.
MEN.   This is strange now: do you two know how you are cen-
  sured here in the city, I mean of us o' the right-hand file? do   20
  you?

6 *who does the wolf love?*] The suggestion is that there are beasts like mobs who love
  nobody.
14 *In what enormity . . . in*] In what fault. The redundant duplication of the preposition
  is not uncommon. Cf. *Rom. and Jul.,* II, *Prol.,* 3: "That fair *for* which love groaned
  for."
19–20 *how you are censured . . . file?*] what opinion is formed of you by us of the supe-
  rior classes? Cf. I, vi, 53, *supra:* "The common *file,*" *i.e.,* the rank and file, and
  Macb., III, i, 94: "the valued *file*" (*i.e.,* the better classes).

29

Both. Why, how are we censured?

Men. Because you talk of pride now,—will you not be angry?

Both. Well, well, sir, well.

Men. Why, 't is no great matter; for a very little thief of occasion
will rob you of a great deal of patience: give your dispositions
the reins, and be angry at your pleasures; at the least, if you
take it as a pleasure to you in being so. You blame Marcius
for being proud?

Bru. We do it not alone, sir.   30

Men. I know you can do very little alone; for your helps are
many, or else your actions would grow wondrous single: your
abilities are too infant-like for doing much alone. You talk of
pride: O that you could turn your eyes toward the napes of
your necks, and make but an interior survey of your good
selves! O that you could!

Both. What then, sir?

Men. Why, then you should discover a brace of unmeriting,
proud, violent, testy magistrates, alias fools, as any in Rome.

Sic. Menenius, you are known well enough too.   40

Men. I am known to be a humorous patrician, and one that
loves a cup of hot wine with not a drop of allaying Tiber in
't; said to be something imperfect in favouring the first complaint, hasty and tinder-like upon too trivial motion; one that
converses more with the buttock of the night than with the
forehead of the morning: what I think I utter, and spend my
malice in my breath. Meeting two such wealsmen as you

32 *single*] a quibble on the two senses of the word; "one" and "weak" or "feeble." Cf. 2
   Hen. IV, I, ii, 173: "your chin double, your wit *single*."
34–35 *the napes of your necks*] an allusion to the vulgar notion that men bore behind
   them a bag in which they stowed their own faults, keeping in front of them a second
   bag for their neighbours' shortcomings.
41 *humorous*] capricious, whimsical.
42 *allaying*] mitigating or diluting. Cf. Lovelace's well-known song "To Althæa from
   prison" (ll. 9–10): "When flowing cups run swiftly round With no *allaying* Thames."
   For "allay" see V, iii, 95, *infra*.
43–44 *something imperfect . . . first complaint*] showing some defect of rashness in taking the part of the first grumbler without waiting to hear another side. For *first complaint* Collier suggested *thirst complaint*.
44 *motion*] provocation.
44–46 *one that converses . . . morning*] one who stays up late rather than rises early. Cf.
   L. L. L., V, i, 76–77: "the *posteriors* of this day which the rude multitude call the
   afternon."
47 *in my breath*] in speech.
47 *wealsmen*] statesmen, men of the state or commonwealth.

are,—I cannot call you Lycurguses—if the drink you give
me touch my palate adversely, I make a crooked face at it. I
can't say your worships have delivered the matter well, when   50
I find the ass in compound with the major part of your syllables: and though I must be content to bear with those that
say you are reverend grave men, yet they lie deadly that tell
you you have good faces. If you see this in the map of my microcosm, follows it that I am known well enough too? what
harm can your bisson conspectuities glean out of this character, if I be known well enough too?

BRU.   Come, sir, come, we know you well enough.

MEN.   You know neither me, yourselves, nor any thing. You are
ambitious for poor knaves' caps and legs: you wear out a   60
good wholesome forenoon in hearing a cause between an
orange-wife and a fosset-seller, and then rejourn the controversy of three-pence to a second day of audience. When you
are hearing a matter between party and party, if you chance
to be pinched with the colic, you make faces like mummers;
set up the bloody flag against all patience; and, in roaring for
a chamber-pot, dismiss the controversy bleeding, the more
entangled by your hearing: all the peace you make in their
cause is, calling both the parties knaves. You are a pair of
strange ones.   70

BRU.   Come, come, you are well understood to be a perfecter
giber for the table than a necessary bencher in the Capitol.

48 *Lycurguses*] Lycurgus was the famous lawgiver of Sparta, whose life was included by
      Plutarch in his collection of biographies.
50 *can't*] Theobald's correction of the Folio reading *can*.
51–52 *I find the ass . . . syllables*] Menenius' meaning is that he finds in almost every-
      thing the tribunes have uttered proofs that they are asses.
54–55 *the map of my microcosm*] the survey of my personality. The phrase reflects the
      language of mystic philosophers who habitually describe man as "a little world," an
      epitome of the universe.
56 *bisson conspectuities*] purblind visions.
59–60 *You are ambitious . . . legs*] You want the obeisances of poor fellows. "To make a
      leg" meant "to make a bow."
60–63 *you wear out . . . audience*] Shakespeare is in error in connecting the tribunes of
      the people with any judicial functions. The police magistrates were the prætors. The
      tribunes only exercised powers of protest or veto in regard to laws and regulations
      promulgated by the superior authorities.
62 *fosset-seller*] seller of spigots, or pegs, which formed part of the taps of beer barrels.
65 *mummers*] masquers.
66 *set up . . . patience*] declare downright war with patience, conduct yourselves with
      the utmost impatience. Cf. *Hen. V*, I, ii, 101: "unwind your *bloody flag*."
67 *bleeding*] raw, unsettled.
72 *a necessary bencher in the Capitol*] a competent magistrate.

MEN. Our very priests must become mockers, if they shall encounter such ridiculous subjects as you are. When you speak
best unto the purpose, it is not worth the wagging of your
beards; and your beards deserve not so honourable a grave as
to stuff a botcher's cushion, or to be entombed in an ass's
pack-saddle. Yet you must be saying, Marcius is proud; who,
in a cheap estimation, is worth all your predecessors since
Deucalion; though peradventure some of the best of 'em   80
were hereditary hangmen. God-den to your worships: more
of your conversation would infect my brain, being the herds-
men of the beastly plebeians: I will be bold to take my leave
of you.   [BRUTUS *and* SICINIUS *go aside.*

Enter VOLUMNIA, VIRGILIA, *and* VALERIA

How now, my as fair as noble ladies,—and the moon, were
she earthly, no nobler—whither do you follow your eyes so
fast?
VOL. Honourable Menenius, my boy Marcius approaches; for
the love of Juno, let's go.
MEN. Ha! Marcius coming home?   90
VOL. Ay, worthy Menenius; and with most prosperous approba-
tion.
MEN. Take my cap, Jupiter, and I thank thee. Hoo! Marcius
coming home?
VIR.
VAL. } Nay, 't is true.
VOL. Look, here's a letter from him: the state hath another, his
wife another; and, I think, there's one at home for you.
MEN. I will make my very house reel to-night: a letter for me?
VIR. Yes, certain, there 's a letter for you; I saw 't.
MEN. A letter for me! it gives me an estate of seven years'   100
health; in which time I will make a lip at the physician: the
most sovereign prescription in Galen is but empiricutic,

75–76 *the wagging of your beards*] the opening of your mouths.
77 *a botcher's cushion*] the pillow which was employed by a jobbing tailor when re-
pairing clothes.
80 *Deucalion*] The Noah of the Deluge in classical mythology. Cf. Ovid's *Metam.*, i,
313 *seq.*
81 *God-den*] good-evening.
101 *make a lip*] make a grimace.
102 *Galen*] the great Greek physician who lived in the second century of the Christian
era, some six hundred years after the date of the present history.
102 *empiricutic*] quack medicine. The word is Menenius' coinage from "empiric."

and, to this preservative, of no better report than a horse-
drench. Is he not wounded? he was wont to come home
wounded.

VIR.   O, no, no, no.

VOL.   O, he is wounded; I thank the gods for 't.

MEN.   So do I too, if it be not too much: brings a' victory in his
pocket? the wounds become him.

VOL.   On 's brows: Menenius, he comes the third time home   110
with the oaken garland.

MEN.   Has he disciplined Aufidius soundly?

VOL.   Titus Lartius writes, they fought together, but Aufidius got
off.

MEN.   And 't was time for him too, I'll warrant him that: an he
had stayed by him, I would not have been so fidiused for all
the chests in Corioli, and the gold that's in them. Is the senate possessed of this?

VOL.   Good ladies, let's go. Yes, yes, yes; the senate has letters
from the general, wherein he gives my son the whole name   120
of the war: he hath in this action outdone his former deeds
doubly.

VAL.   In troth, there's wondrous things spoke of him.

MEN.   Wondrous! ay, I warrant you, and not without his true
purchasing.

VIR.   The gods grant them true!

VOL.   True! pow, wow.

MEN.   True! I'll be sworn they are true. Where is he wounded?
[*To the* Tribunes] God save your good worships! Marcius is
coming home: he has more cause to be proud. Where is he   130
wounded?

VOL.   I' the shoulder and i' the left arm: there will be large ci-
catrices to show the people, when he shall stand for his
place. He received in the repulse of Tarquin seven hurts i'
the body.

---

103 *to this*] compared to this.

111 *the oaken garland*] Cf. I, iii, 13, *supra*, and note.

116 *fidiused*] a verb jocularly coined from the name "Aufidius." It means here "whipped
(or beaten) as Aufidius was."

118 *possessed*] fully informed.

120 *the whole name*] the whole credit.

133–134 *for his place*] for the consulship. Volumnia takes for granted that he has won
his right to candidature for the office.

MEN.   One i' the neck, and two i' the thigh; there's nine that I
    know.
VOL.   He had, before this last expedition, twenty five wounds
    upon him.
MEN.   Now it's twenty seven: every gash was an enemy's grave.   140
    [*A shout and flourish.*] Hark! the trumpets.
VOL.   These are the ushers of Marcius: before him
    He carries noise, and behind him he leaves tears:
    Death, that dark spirit, in 's nervy arm doth lie;
    Which, being advanced, declines, and then men die.

A *sennet. Trumpets sound. Enter* COMINIUS *and* TITUS LARTIUS;
    between them, CORIOLANUS, *crowned with an oaken gar-*
    land; with Captains *and* Soldiers, *and a* Herald

HER.   Know, Rome, that all alone Marcius did fight
    Within Corioli gates: where he hath won,
    With fame, a name to Caius Marcius; these
    In honour follows Coriolanus.
    Welcome to Rome, renowned Coriolanus!   [*Flourish.*   150
ALL.   Welcome to Rome, renowned Coriolanus!
COR.   No more of this, it does offend my heart;
    Pray now, no more.
COM.   Look, sir, your mother!
COR.   O,
    You have, I know, petition'd all the gods
    For my prosperity!   [*Kneels.*
VOL.   Nay, my good soldier, up;
    My gentle Marcius, worthy Caius, and
    By deed-achieving honour newly named,—   160
    What is it?—Coriolanus must I call thee?—
    But, O, thy wife!

136–137 *there's nine that I know*] Menenius counts in silence after enumerating the sec-
    ond wound, and then announces a total of nine wounds within his knowledge.
144 *nervy*] sinewy.
145 *Which, being advanced*] Which, being merely raised up and let fall, causes men to
    die.
145 *A sennet*] A note on the trumpet, announcing the entry of a distinguished person.
    (stage direction)
145 *Titus Lartius*] This character was ordered to Corioli, I, ix, 82–83, *supra*, and is sent
    for thence, II, ii, 34–35, *infra*, so that he could not have been in Rome on the oc-
    casion of Coriolanus' triumph. His name seems mentioned in error. No word is al-
    lotted him in this scene.
148 *a name to*] a name in addition to.

COR.   My gracious silence, hail!
    Wouldst thou have laugh'd had I come coffin'd home,
    That weep'st to see me triumph? Ah, my dear,
    Such eyes the widows in Corioli wear,
    And mothers that lack sons.
MEN.   Now, the gods crown thee!
COR.   And live you yet? [*To* VALERIA] O my sweet lady, pardon.
VOL.   I know not where to turn: O, welcome home: 170
    And welcome, general: and ye're welcome all.
MEN.   A hundred thousand welcomes. I could weep,
    And I could laugh; I am light and heavy. Welcome:
    A curse begin at very root on's heart,
    That is not glad to see thee! You are three
    That Rome should dote on: yet, by the faith of men,
    We have some old crab-trees here at home that will not
    Be grafted to your relish. Yet welcome, warriors:
    We call a nettle but a nettle, and
    The faults of fools but folly.   180
COM.   Ever right.
COR.   Menenius, ever, ever.
HER.   Give way there, and go on.
COR. [*To* VOLUMNIA *and* VIRGILIA]   Your hand, and yours:
    Ere in our own house I do shade my head,
    The good patricians must be visited;
    From whom I have received not only greetings,
    But with them change of honours.
VOL.   _   I have lived
    To see inherited my very wishes   190
    And the buildings of my fancy: only
    There's one thing wanting, which I doubt not but
    Our Rome will cast upon thee.
COR.   Know, good mother,
    I had rather be their servant in my way
    Than sway with them in theirs.
COM.   O, to the Capitol!

                    [*Flourish. Cornets. Exeunt in state,
            as before* BRUTUS *and* SICINIUS *come forward.*

163 *My gracious silence, hail!*] The hero half ironically compliments his gentle wife on
    her tearful silence.
182 *Menenius, ever, ever*] Menenius is still the same frank old friend that he always was.
188 *with them change of honours*] with the greetings varieties of honours. Theobald pro-
    posed to substitute *charge* (*i.e.,* responsibility) for *change*.

Bru.   All tongues speak of him, and the bleared sights
    Are spectacled to see him: your prattling nurse
    Into a rapture lets her baby cry   200
    While she chats him: the kitchen malkin pins
    Her richest lockram 'bout her reechy neck,
    Clambering the walls to eye him: stalls, bulks, windows,
    Are smother'd up, leads fill'd and ridges horsed
    With variable complexions, all agreeing
    In earnestness to see him: seld-shown flamens
    Do press among the popular throngs, and puff
    To win a vulgar station: our veil'd dames
    Commit the war of white and damask in
    Their nicely-gawded cheeks to the wanton spoil   210
    Of Phœbus' burning kisses: such a pother,
    As if that whatsoever god who leads him
    Were silly crept into his human powers,
    And gave him graceful posture.
Sic.   On the sudden,
    I warrant him consul.
Bru.   Then our office may,
    During his power, go sleep.
Sic.   He cannot temperately transport his honours
    From where he should begin and end, but will   220
    Lose those he hath won.

200 *rapture*] seizure or paroxysm.
201 *chats him*] makes Coriolanus the subject of her chat.
201 *kitchen malkin*] kitchen slut or slattern. "Malkin" is properly the diminutive of "Mall" or "Mary."
202 *lockram . . . reechy*] cheap linen . . . reeking, greasy.
203 *bulks*] boards or ledges fastened to the outside of a house, on which articles were offered for sale.
204–205 *ridges horsed . . . complexions*] roof-tops ridden astride by men and women of all sorts and conditions.
206 *self-shown flamens*] priests who seldom appear in public.
208 *a vulgar station*] a place among the common people.
208–211 *our veil'd dames . . . burning kisses*] a stilted way of saying that the women risk letting their pink and white complexions be spoiled by sunburn. Woman's cheeks were commonly credited by Elizabethan poets with being the battleground of white and red colours. Cf. *T. of Shrew*, IV, v, 30: "Such *war of white and red* within her *cheek*."
210 *nicely-gawded*] prettily ornamented.
212 *whatsoever god*] the god whoever he be; an allusion to the demon or guardian angel who was commonly reckoned to find a home in each man's soul and to direct his conduct.
219–221 *He cannot . . . won*] He cannot moderately proceed through the progressive grades of honour from the first stage to the last, but will sacrifice by his impetuosity the honours he gains by the way.

BRU.   In that there's comfort.
SIC.   Doubt not
    The commoners, for whom we stand, but they
    Upon their ancient malice will forget
    With the least cause these his new honours; which
    That he will give them make I as little question
    As he is proud to do 't.
BRU.   I heard him swear,
    Were he to stand for consul, never would he   230
    Appear i' the market-place, nor on him put
    The napless vesture of humility,
    Nor showing, as the manner is, his wounds
    To the people, beg their stinking breaths.
SIC.   'T is right.
BRU.   It was his word: O, he would miss it rather
    Than carry it but by the suit of the gentry to him,
    And the desire of the nobles.
SIC.   I wish no better
    Than have him hold that purpose and to put it   240
    In execution.
BRU.   'T is most like he will.
SIC.   It shall be to him then, as our good wills,
    A sure destruction.
BRU.   So it must fall out
    To him or our authorities. For an end,
    We must suggest the people in what hatred
    He still hath held them; that to 's power he would
    Have made them mules, silenced their pleaders and
    Dispropertied their freedoms; holding them,   250
    In human action and capacity,
    Of no more soul nor fitness for the world

225 *Upon their ancient malice*] Owing to their old hatred.
226–228 *which That . . . to do 't*] and make no question but that he will give the people
    reason (for forgetting his new honours), and that he will feel pride in provoking
    their forgetfulness.
232 *The napless vesture of humility*] The poor threadbare garment of humility, which
    candidates for office in Republican Rome were compelled to wear.
234 *breaths*] suffrages, votes.
243–244 *It shall be . . . sure destruction*] It shall be to him then, as our best wishes would
    have it, certain ruin.
247 *suggest*] prompt.
248 *to 's power*] as far as his power went.
250 *Dispropertied their freedoms*] Dispossessed, or deprived, them of their liberties.
252 *Of no more soul . . . world*] Of no more intelligent feeling nor use in the world.

Than camels in the war, who have their provand
Only for bearing burthens, and sore blows
For sinking under them.
SIC.   This, as you say, suggested
At some time when his soaring insolence
Shall touch the people—which time shall not want,
If he be put upon 't; and that 's as easy
As to set dogs on sheep—will be his fire   260
To kindle their dry stubble; and their blaze
Shall darken him for ever.

Enter a Messenger

BRU.   What 's the matter?
MESS.   You are sent for to the Capitol. 'T is thought
That Marcius shall be consul:
I have seen the dumb men throng to see him and
The blind to hear him speak: matrons flung gloves,
Ladies and maids their scarfs and handkerchers,
Upon him as he pass'd: the nobles bended,
As to Jove's statue, and the commons made   270
A shower and thunder with their caps and shouts:
I never saw the like.
BRU.   Let 's to the Capitol,
And carry with us ears and eyes for the time,
But hearts for the event.
SIC.   Have with you.   [*Exeunt.*

SCENE II. *The Same. The Capitol.*

Enter two Officers, *to lay cushions*

FIRST OFF.   Come, come, they are almost here. How many
stand for consulships?

---

253 *provand*] an exceptional form of "provender."
258 *touch*] Hanmer's change for the Folio reading *teach*. Pope read *reach*. "Teach the
     people" might possibly mean "Put them in the appropriate frame of mind."
259 *put upon 't*] roused to anger.
260 *his fire*] as a fire lighted by himself.
271 *with their caps*] by flinging up their caps which came down showerwise.
274 *carry with us . . . event*] keep our eyes and ears open for all that is passing and keep
     our hearts resolute in regard to the issue.
276 *Have with you*] Get along.

SEC. OFF.   Three, they say: but 't is thought of every one
Coriolanus will carry it.

FIRST OFF.   That 's a brave fellow; but he 's vengeance proud,
and loves not the common people.

SEC. OFF.   Faith, there have been many great men that have
flattered the people, who ne'er loved them; and there be
many that they have loved, they know not wherefore: so that,
if they love they know not why, they hate upon no better a   10
ground: therefore, for Coriolanus neither to care whether
they love or hate him manifests the true knowledge he has
in their disposition; and out of his noble carelessness lets
them plainly see 't.

FIRST OFF.   If he did not care whether he had their love or no,
he waved indifferently 'twixt doing them neither good nor
harm: but he seeks their hate with greater devotion than they
can render it him, and leaves nothing undone that may fully
discover him their opposite. Now, to seem to affect the malice and displeasure of the people is as bad as that which he   20
dislikes, to flatter them for their love.

SEC. OFF.   He hath deserved worthily of his country: and his ascent is not by such easy degrees as those who, having been
supple and courteous to the people, bonneted, without any
further deed to have them at all into their estimation and report: but he hath so planted his honours in their eyes and his
actions in their hearts, that for their tongues to be silent and
not confess so much, were a kind of ingrateful injury; to report otherwise were a malice that, giving itself the lie, would
pluck reproof and rebuke from every ear that heard it.   30

FIRST OFF.   No more of him; he 's a worthy man: make way,
they are coming.

A sennet. *Enter, with* Lictors *before them,* COMINIUS *the Consul,*
MENENIUS, CORIOLANUS, Senators, SICINIUS *and* BRUTUS.
The Senators *take their places; the* Tribunes *take their*
places by themselves. CORIOLANUS *stands.*

5 *he's vengeance proud*] he's proud with a vengeance, excessively proud.
16 *he waved indifferently*] he would have been quite neutral; he would have shown indifference.
17 *devotion*] earnestness.
19 *opposite*] enemy, opponent.
19 *affect*] attract, pursue.
23 *by such easy degrees as those*] by such easy stages as the ascent of those.
24–25 *bonneted . . . estimation*] took off their caps (to the people) and so won their way
into the people's estimation and repute, without doing anything else to get into their
favour or regard.

MEN.   Having determined of the Volsces and
    To send for Titus Lartius, it remains,
    As the main point of this our after-meeting,
    To gratify his noble service that
    Hath thus stood for his country: therefore, please you,
    Most reverend and grave elders, to desire
    The present consul, and last general
    In our well-found successes, to report   40
    A little of that worthy work perform'd
    By Caius Marcius Coriolanus; whom
    We met here, both to thank and to remember
    With honours like himself.
FIRST SEN.   Speak, good Cominius:
    Leave nothing out for length, and make us think
    Rather our state 's defective for requital
    Than we to stretch it out. [*To the* Tribunes] Masters o' the
       people,
    We do request your kindest ears, and after,
    Your loving motion toward the common body,   50
    To yield what passes here.
SIC.   We are convented
    Upon a pleasing treaty, and have hearts
    Inclinable to honour and advance
    The theme of our assembly.
BRU.   Which the rather
    We shall be bless'd to do, if he remember
    A kinder value of the people than
    He hath hereto prized them at.
MEN.   That 's off, that 's off;   60
    I would you rather had been silent. Please you
    To hear Cominius speak?
BRU.   Most willingly:

43–44 *to remember With honours like himself*] to recommemorate with honours pro-
    portionate to his merits.
46–48 *make us think . . . stretch it out*] make us think that the republic is rather too
    niggardly in rewarding his service than suppose us to exaggerate the merits of his ser-
    vice.
49 *your kindest ears*] your most favourable attention.
50 *Your loving . . . body*] Your kind interposition with the populace.
51 *yield*] announce.
52 *convented*] convened.
57 *bless'd to do*] happy in doing.
59 *prized*] valued.
60 *That's off*] That's off the point, irrelevant.

    But yet my caution was more pertinent
    Than the rebuke you give it.
MEN.   He loves your people;
    But tie him not to be their bedfellow.
    Worthy Cominius, speak. [CORIOLANUS *offers to go away.*]
      Nay, keep your place.
FIRST SEN.   Sit, Coriolanus; never shame to hear
    What you have nobly done.   70
COR.   Your honours' pardon:
    I had rather have my wounds to heal again,
    Than hear say how I got them.
BRU.   Sir, I hope
    My words disbench'd you not.
COR.   No, sir: yet oft,
    When blows have made me stay, I fled from words.
    You sooth'd not, therefore hurt not: but your people,
    I love them as they weigh.
MEN.   Pray now, sit down.   80
COR.   I had rather have one scratch my head i' the sun
    When the alarum were stuck than idly sit
    To hear my nothings monster'd.   •   [*Exit.*
MEN.   Masters of the people,
    Your multiplying spawn how can he flatter—
    That's thousand to one good one—when you now see
    He had rather venture all his limbs for honour
    Than one on 's ears to hear it?   Proceed, Cominius.
COM.   I shall lack voice: the deeds of Coriolanus
    Should not be utter'd feebly. It is held   90
    That valour is the chiefest virtue and
    Most dignifies the haver: if it be,
    The man I speak of cannot in the world
    Be singly counterpoised. At sixteen years,
    When Tarquin made a head for Rome, he fought
    Beyond the mark of others: our then dictator,

---

75 *disbench'd you*] caused you to leave your seat or bench.
78 *sooth'd*] flattered.
79 *weigh*] merit.
83 *monster'd*] grossly exaggerated.
86 *That's thousand . . . one*] There is but one good man in a thousand of such riffraff.
95 *made a head for Rome*] raised an army to reconquer Rome.
96 *our then dictator*] Vague hints of Plutarch are followed here: "Marcius valiantly
    fought in the sight of the Dictator." The dictator is not identified by Plutarch.
    According to Livy, Titus Lartius was the first Roman to be made dictator. He was ap-
    pointed during the war with the Tarquins.

Whom with all praise I point at, saw him fight,
When with his Amazonian chin he drove
The bristled lips before him: he bestrid
An o'er-press'd Roman, and i' the consul's view   100
Slew three opposers: Tarquin's self he met,
And struck him on his knee: in that day's feats,
When he might act the woman in the scene,
He proved best man i' the field, and for his meed
Was brow-bound with the oak. His pupil age
Man-enter'd thus, he waxed like a sea;
And, in the brunt of seventeen battles since,
He lurch'd all swords of the garland. For this last,
Before and in Corioli, let me say,
I cannot speak him home: he stopp'd the fliers;   110
And by his rare example made the coward
Turn terror into sport: as weeds before
A vessel under sail, so men obey'd,
And fell below his stem: his sword, death's stamp,
Where it did mark, it took; from face to foot
He was a thing of blood, whose every motion
Was timed with dying cries: alone he enter'd

98 *Amazonian chin*] beardless chin.

99 *bestrid*] saved a man's life in battle by standing astride of him. It was always reckoned one of the most honourable of services. Cf. *Macb.*, IV, iii, 4: "like good men
Bestride our down-fall'n birthdom."

102 *struck him on his knee*] with a sudden blow brought him to his knee.

103 *When he might act the woman*] a reference to the practice of boys taking women's
parts on the contemporary stage.

105 *brow-bound with the oak*] See note on I, iii, 13, *supra.*

105–106 *His pupil age Man-enter'd thus*] The general sense is that his minority was distinguished by all the virtues and valour of manhood.

108 *He lurch'd all swords of the garland*] Cf. Ben Jonson's Silent Woman, V, iv, 227:
"You have lurch'd [i.e., deprived, cheated] your friends of the better halfe of the garland." "Lurch" was a term familiar to card-players and card-sharpers, and connoted
great rapidity in the deceptive operation. There was a card game so called, and the
word was often applied to a victory in any set or rubber in which no points were
scored by the adversary.

112 *weeds*] Thus the First Folio, for which later Folios substitute *waves.* "Weeds" con-
fuses the metaphor, but may well be retained, since it emphasises the feebleness of
Coriolanus' enemy.

114 *his sword, death's stamp*] the instrument with which death sealed or stamped men
for its own.

115 *Where it did mark, it took*] It took effect wherever it touched.

116–117 *every motion . . . cries*] the cries of the slaughtered followed his movement with
the regularity with which a dancer keeps time to the music.

    ·   The mortal gate of the city, which he painted
With shunless destiny; aidless came off,
And with a sudden re-enforcement struck   120
Corioli like a planet: now all 's his:
When, by and by, the din of war gan pierce
His ready sense; then straight his doubled spirit
Re-quicken'd what in flesh was fatigate,
And to the battle came he; where he did
Run reeking o'er the lives of men, as if
'T were a perpetual spoil: and till we call'd
Both field and city ours, he never stood
To ease his breast with panting.
MEN.   Worthy man!   130
FIRST SEN.   He cannot but with measure fit the honours
    Which we devise him.
COM.   Our spoils he kick'd at,
    And look'd upon things precious, as they were
    The common muck of the world: he covets less
    Than misery itself would give; rewards
    His deeds with doing them, and is content
    To spend the time to end it.
MEN.   He 's right noble:
    Let him be call'd for.   140
FIRST SEN.   Call Coriolanus.
OFF.   He doth appear.

Re-enter CORIOLANUS

MEN.   The senate, Coriolanus, are well pleased
    To make thee consul.
COR.   I do owe them still
    My life and services.
MEN.   It then remains
    That you do speak to the people.

118–119 *The mortal gate . . . destiny*] The gate of the city doomed to destruction, which
    he covered with the blood of those destined to death without chance of escape.
120–121 *struck Corioli like a planet*] an allusion to the sudden fatalities ascribed to plan-
    etary influence.
124 *fatigate*] wearied out.
131 *with measure*] with propriety, competently.
133 *kick'd at*] spurned.
136 *misery*] parsimony, avarice. The word is formed from "miser."
138 *To spend . . . to end it*] To spend the time in doing great acts for their own sake and
    not for the sake of future reward. "To end" has the sense of "to finish up altogether,"
    "to have done with."

COR.   I do beseech you,
 Let me o'erleap that custom, for I cannot   150
 Put on the gown, stand naked, and entreat them,
 For my wounds' sake, to give their suffrage: please you
 That I may pass this doing.
SIC.   Sir, the people
 Must have their voices; neither will they bate
 One jot of ceremony.
MEN.   Put them not to 't:
 Pray you, go fit you to the custom, and
 Take to you, as your predecessors have,
 Your honour with your form.   160
COR.   It is a part
 That I shall blush in acting, and might well
 Be taken from the people.
BRU.   Mark you that?
COR. To brag unto them, thus I did, and thus;
 Show them the unaching scars which I should hide,
 As if I had received them for the hire
 Of their breath only!
MEN.   Do not stand upon 't.
 We recommend to you, tribunes of the people, 170
 Our purpose to them: and to our noble consul
 Wish we all joy and honour.
SENATORS. To Coriolanus come all joy and honour!

 [*Flourish of cornets. Exeunt all but* SICINIUS *and* BRUTUS.

BRU. You see how he intends to use the people.

150–151 *that custom . . . entreat them*] according to North's rendering of Plutarch's *Life of Coriolanus:* "it was the custome of Rome at that time, that such as dyd sue for any office, should for certen dayes before be in the market-place, only with a poor gowne on their backes, and without any coate underneath, to praye the people to remember them at the day of election."
153 *pass this doing*] omit this action.
155 *have their voices*] exercise their votes. The term "voice" was invariably used for "vote" by Shakespeare.
157 *Put them not to 't*] Do not rouse their anger.
160 *with your form*] in the manner prescribed for you by tradition.
169 *Do not stand upon 't*] Do not be obstinate.
170–171 *We recommend . . . to them*] We ask you tribunes of the people to recommend to the plebeians for their approbation what we are proposing to them, *viz.*, Coriolanus' appointment to the consulship.

Sic.   May they perceive 's intent! He will require them,
        As if he did contemn what he requested
        Should be in them to give.
Bru.   Come, we'll inform them
        Of our proceedings here: on the market-place,
        I know, they do attend us.   [*Exeunt.*   180

SCENE III. *The Same. The Forum.*

Enter seven or eight Citizens

First Cit.   Once, if he do require our voices, we ought not to
        deny him.
Sec. Cit.   We may, sir, if we will.
Third Cit.   We have power in ourselves to do it, but it is a
        power that we have no power to do: for if he show us his
        wounds and tell us his deeds, we are to put our tongues into
        those wounds and speak for them; so, if he tell us his noble
        deeds, we must also tell him our noble acceptance of them.
        Ingratitude is monstrous: and for the multitude to be in-
        grateful, were to make a monster of the multitude; of the   10
        which we being members, should bring ourselves to be
        monstrous members.
First Cit.   And to make us no better thought of, a little help
        will serve; for once we stood up about the corn, he himself
        stuck not to call us the many-headed multitude.
Third Cit.   We have been called so of many; not that our heads
        are some brown, some black, some auburn, some bald, but
        that our wits are so diversely coloured: and truly I think, if all
        our wits were to issue out of one skull, they would fly east,
        west, north, south, and their consent of one direct way   20
        should be at once to all the points o' the compass.
Sec. Cit.   Think you so? Which way do you judge my wit
        would fly?

175–177 *He will require . . . to give*] He will make demand of them, as if he scorned the
    fact that it should be in their power to give him what he requested.
180 *attend*] wait for. Cf. I, x, 32, *supra.*

    1 *Once*] Once for all, in a word.
    4–5 *it is a power . . . power to do*] it is a natural power that we have no moral right to
        exercise. "Power" is used in two different senses.
    14 *once we stood up*] no sooner did we stand up (than).
    17 *auburn*] Thus the Fourth Folio.

THIRD CIT.   Nay, your wit will not so soon out as another man's
    will; 't is strongly wedged up in a blockhead; but if it were at
    liberty, 't would, sure, southward.
SEC. CIT.   Why that way?
THIRD CIT.   To lose itself in a fog; where being three parts
    melted away with rotten dews, the fourth would return for
    conscience sake, to help to get thee a wife.   30
SEC. CIT.   You are never without your tricks: you may, you may.
THIRD CIT.   Are you all resolved to give your voices? But that's
    no matter, the greater part carries it. I say, if he would in-
    cline to the people, there was never a worthier man.

Enter CORIOLANUS *in a gown of humility, with* MENENIUS

    Here he comes, and in the gown of humility: mark his be-
    haviour. We are not to stay all together, but to come by him
    where he stands, by ones, by twos, and by threes. He 's to
    make his requests by particulars; wherein every one of us has
    a single honour, in giving him our own voices with our own
    tongues: therefore follow me, and I'll direct you how you   40
    shall go by him.
ALL.   Content, content.   [*Exeunt* Citizens.
MEN.   O sir, you are not right: have you not known
    The worthiest men have done 't?
COR.   What must I say?—
    "I pray, sir,"—Plague upon 't! I cannot bring
    My tongue to such a pace. "Look, sir, my wounds!
    I got them in my country's service, when
    Some certain of your brethren roar'd, and ran
    From the noise of our own drums."   50
MEN.   O me, the gods!
    You must not speak of that: you must desire them
    To think upon you.
COR.   Think upon me! hang 'em!
    I would they would forget me, like the virtues
    Which our divines lose by 'em.

26 *southward*] The south wind is invariably described by Shakespeare as bringing fog
    and rain. Cf. I, iv, 35, *supra*, and *As you like it*, III, v, 50: "Like foggy *south*, puffing
    with wind and rain."
31 *you may, you may*] please go on; used ironically.
38 *by particulars*] addressing each of us individually.
53 *To think upon you*] To think well of you.
55 *like the virtues . . . by 'em*] As they forget the virtuous teachings which our divines
    waste on them, or lose their time by preaching to them.

MEN.   You 'll mar all:
    I 'll leave you: pray you, speak to 'em, I pray you,
    In wholesome manner.   [*Exit.*
COR.   Bid them wash their faces,   60
    And keep their teeth clean. [*Re-enter two of the* Citizens.]
      So, here comes a brace.

Re-enter a third Citizen

    You know the cause, sir, of my standing here.
THIRD CIT.   We do, sir; tell us what hath brought you to 't.
COR.   Mine own desert.
SEC. CIT.   Your own desert!
COR.   Ay, but not mine own desire.
THIRD CIT.   How! not your own desire!
COR.   No, sir, 't was never my desire yet to trouble the poor with
    begging.
THIRD CIT.   You must think, if we give you any thing, we hope   70
    to gain by you.
COR.   Well then, I pray, your price o' the consulship?
FIRST CIT.   The price is, to ask it kindly.
COR.   Kindly! Sir, I pray, let me ha 't: I have wounds to show
    you, which shall be yours in private. Your good voice, sir;
    what say you?
SEC. CIT.   You shall ha 't, worthy sir.
COR.   A match, sir. There 's in all two worthy voices begged. I
    have your alms: adieu.
THIRD CIT.   But this is something odd.   80
SEC. CIT.   An 't were to give again,—but 't is no matter.
                     [*Exeunt the three* Citizens.

Re-enter two other Citizens

COR.   Pray you now, if it may stand with the tune of your voices
    that I may be consul, I have here the customary gown.
FOURTH CIT.   You have deserved nobly of your country, and you
    have not deserved nobly.
COR.   Your enigma?
FOURTH CIT.   You have been a scourge to her enemies, you
    have been a rod to her friends; you have not indeed loved
    the common people.

---

66 *Ay, but not mine*] The First Folio erroneously omits *not*. The other Folios (substantially) omit *but*. The presence of the two words improves the sense.

COR.   You should account me the more virtuous, that I have not   90
    been common in my love. I will, sir, flatter my sworn
    brother, the people, to earn a dearer estimation of them; 't is
    a condition they account gentle: and since the wisdom of
    their choice is rather to have my hat than my heart, I will
    practise the insinuating nod, and be off to them most coun-
    terfeitly; that is, sir, I will counterfeit the bewitchment of
    some popular man, and give it bountiful to the desirers.
    Therefore, beseech you, I may be consul.

FIFTH CIT.   We hope to find you our friend; and therefore give
    you our voices heartily.   100

FOURTH CIT.   You have received many wounds for your country.

COR.   I will not seal your knowledge with showing them. I will
    make much of your voices, and so trouble you no farther.

BOTH CIT.   The gods give you joy, sir, heartily!   [*Exeunt.*

COR.   Most sweet voices!
    Better it is to die, better to starve,
    Than crave the hire which first we do deserve.
    Why in this woolvish toge should I stand here,
    To beg of Hob and Dick that do appear,
    Their needless vouches? Custom calls me to 't: 110
    What custom wills, in all things should we do 't,
    The dust on antique time would lie unswept,
    And mountainous error be too highly heap'd
    For truth to o'er-peer. Rather than fool it so,
    Let the high office and the honour go
    To one that would do thus. I am half through:
    The one part suffer'd, the other will I do.

Re-enter three Citizens *more*

91–92 *sworn brother*] bosom friend, comrade in adventurous enterprise; a reference to the
    mediæval institution of "fratres jurati," men bound by oath to share together chivalric
    adventures. Cf. *Rich. II*, V, i, 20–21: "I am *sworn brother* . . . To grim Necessity."
92 *to earn . . . of them*] to earn of them a higher opinion.
93 *a condition*] the sort of behaviour.
95 *be off to them most counterfeitly*] take my hat off to them with a pretence of real feel-
    ing.
96 *bewitchment*] bewitching address. Cf. *Hen. VIII*, III, ii, 18–19: "he hath a *witchcraft*
    . . . in 's tongue."
102 *seal*] complete, give the final touch to.
106 *starve*] Thus the Fourth Folio. The earlier Folios give the old form *sterve*, which the
    rhyme with *deserve* seems to require.
108 *toge*] Thus Steevens and Malone. The First Folio reads *tongue*; the later Folios
    gowne. "Toge" (*i.e.*, toga) is doubtless right.
109 *Hob and Dick*] common names of country bumpkins.
110 *vouches*] voices, votes.

Here come moe voices.
Your voices: for your voices I have fought;
Watch'd for your voices; for your voices bear   120
Of wounds two dozen odd; battles thrice six
I have seen, and heard of; for your voices have
Done many things, some less, some more: your voices:
Indeed, I would be consul.

SIXTH CIT.   He has done nobly, and cannot go without any honest man's voice.

SEVENTH CIT.   Therefore let him be consul: the gods give him
joy, and make him good friend to the people!

ALL.   Amen, amen. God save thee, noble consul!   [*Exeunt.*

COR.   Worthy voices!   130

Re-enter MENENIUS, *with* BRUTUS *and* SICINIUS

MEN.   You have stood your limitation; and the tribunes
Endue you with the people's voice: remains
That in the official marks invested you
Anon do meet the senate.

COR.   Is this done?

SIC.   The custom of request you have discharged:
The people do admit you, and are summon'd
To meet anon upon your approbation.

COR.   Where? at the senate-house?

SIC.   There, Coriolanus.   140

COR.   May I change these garments?

SIC.   You may, sir.

COR.   That I'll straight do, and, knowing myself again,
Repair to the senate-house.

MEN.   I'll keep you company. Will you along?

BRU.   We stay here for the people.

SIC.   Fare you well.
                    [*Exeunt* CORIOLANUS *and* MENENIUS.
He has it now; and, by his looks, methinks
'T is warm at 's heart.

---

118 *moe*] an archaic form of "more."
122 *heard of*] The speaker is in an ironical mood. He means that he has heard some
    such talk as that. Cf. II, ii, 107, *supra,* where Cominius credits Coriolanus with "sev-
    enteen" (and not "thrice six," *i.e.,* eighteen) battles.
131–132 *You have stood your limitation . . . people's voice*] You have stood your ap-
    pointed time, and the tribunes invest you with what the people have voted you.
133 *the official marks*] the distinctive badges of office.
149 *'T is warm at 's heart*] It is comforting to his heart.

BRU.   With a proud heart he wore   150
    His humble weeds. Will you dismiss the people?

Re-enter Citizens

SIC.   How now, my masters! have you chose this man?
FIRST CIT.   He has our voices, sir.
BRU.   We pray the gods he may deserve your loves.
SEC. CIT.   Amen, sir: to my poor unworthy notice,
    He mock'd us when he begg'd our voices.
THIRD CIT.   Certainly
    He flouted us downright.
FIRST CIT.   No, 't is his kind of speech; he did not mock us.
SEC. CIT.   Not one amongst us, save yourself, but says   160
    He used us scornfully: he should have show'd us
    His marks of merit, wounds received for 's country.
SIC.   Why, so he did, I am sure.
CITIZENS.   No, no; no man saw 'em.
THIRD CIT.   He said he had wounds which he could show in pri-
    vate;
    And with his hat, thus waving it in scorn,
    "I would be consul," says he: "aged custom,
    But by your voices, will not so permit me;
    Your voices therefore." When we granted that,
    Here was "I thank you for your voices: thank you: 170
    Your most sweet voices: now you have left your voices,
    I have no further with you." Was not this mockery?
SIC.   Why, either were you ignorant to see 't,
    Or, seeing it, of such childish friendliness
    To yield your voices?
BRU.   Could you not have told him,
    As you were lesson'd, when he had no power,
    But was a petty servant to the state,
    He was your enemy; ever spake against
    Your liberties and the charters that you bear   180
    I' the body of the weal: and now, arriving
    A place of potency and sway o' the state,
    If he should still malignantly remain
    Fast foe to the plebeii, your voices might

---

167 *aged custom*] Shakespeare seems to have overlooked the fact that the consular elec-
    tion was really an innovation after the very recent expulsion of the kings.
173 *were you ignorant to see 't*] you lacked the knowledge or intelligence to discern it.
177 *lesson'd*] instructed.
181 *arriving*] reaching. The usage is common.

    Be curses to yourselves? You should have said,
    That as his worthy deeds did claim no less
    Than what he stood for, so his gracious nature
    Would think upon you for your voices, and
    Translate his malice towards you into love,
    Standing your friendly lord. 190

SIC.   Thus to have said,
    As you were fore-advised, had touch'd his spirit
    And tried his inclination; from him pluck'd
    Either his gracious promise, which you might,
    As cause had call'd you up, have held him to;
    Or else it would have gall'd his surly nature,
    Which easily endures not article
    Tying him to aught: so, putting him to rage,
    You should have ta'en the advantage of his choler,
    And pass'd him unelected. 200

BRU.   Did you perceive
    He did solicit you in free contempt
    When he did need your loves; and do you think
    That his contempt shall not be bruising to you
    When he hath power to crush? Why, had your bodies
    No heart among you? or had you tongues to cry
    Against the rectorship of judgement?

SIC.   Have you,
    Ere now, denied the asker? and now again,
    Of him that did not ask but mock, bestow 210
    Your sued-for tongues?

THIRD CIT.   He's not confirm'd; we may deny him yet.
SEC. CIT.   And will deny him:
    I'll have five hundred voices of that sound.
FIRST CIT.   I twice five hundred, and their friends to piece 'em.
BRU.   Get you hence instantly, and tell those friends,
    They have chose a consul that will from them take
    Their liberties, make them of no more voice

---

188 *think upon you for your voices*] retain grateful remembrance of you for your votes.
192 *touch'd*] tested as with the touchstone.
197 *endures not . . . to aught*] does not submit to any binding terms.
202 *free contempt*] unrestrained scorn.
206–207 *or had you tongues . . . of judgement*] or can it be that your tongues express
    themselves in opposition to the rule of judgment? did you vote against your better
    judgment?
211 *Your sued-for tongues*] The votes which should have been solicited of you.
215 *to piece 'em*] to add to them, strengthen them.

Than dogs that are as often beat for barking,
As therefore kept to do so.　　　　　　　　　　　220
SIC.　　　　　　　　　　　　　Let them assemble;
And, on a safer judgement, all revoke
Your ignorant election: enforce his pride
And his old hate unto you: besides, forget not
With what contempt he wore the humble weed,
How in his suit he scorn'd you: but your loves,
Thinking upon his services, took from you
The apprehension of his present portance,
Which most gibingly, ungravely, he did fashion
After the inveterate hate he bears you.　　　　　　230
BRU.　　　　　　　　　　　　　　　　Lay
A fault on us, your tribunes; that we labour'd,
No impediment between, but that you must
Cast your election on him.
SIC.　　　　　　　　　　　　Say, you chose him
More after our commandment than as guided
By your own true affections; and that your minds,
Pre-occupied with what you rather must do
Than what you should, made you against the grain
To voice him consul: lay the fault on us.　　　　　240
BRU.　　Ay, spare us not. Say we read lectures to you,
How youngly he began to serve his country,
How long continued; and what stock he springs of,
The noble house o' the Marcians, from whence came
That Ancus Marcius, Numa's daughter's son,
Who, after great Hostilius, here was king;
Of the same house Publius and Quintus were,
That our best water brought by conduits hither;
And [Censorinus] nobly named so,
Twice being [by the people chosen] censor,　　　　250
Was his great ancestor.

---

220 *As therefore kept to do so*] As kept for the very purpose of doing so.
223 *enforce*] urge, lay stress on; with a sense of deliberate exaggeration. Cf. III, iii, 3,
　　infra: "*Enforce* him with his envy to the people."
228 *portance*] carriage, bearing.
229 *ungravely*] without dignity, extravagantly.
232–234 *we labour'd . . . election on him*] we took pains to remove any obstacle or im-
　　pediment in the way of your inclination to vote for him.
240 *To voice him*] To vote him.
244–251 *The noble house . . . great ancestor*] This account of Coriolanus' ancestry is
　　drawn verbatim from the opening sentences of Plutarch's "Lives."

SIC.   One thus descended,
        That hath beside well in his person wrought
        To be set high in place, we did commend
        To your remembrances: but you have found,
        Scaling his present bearing with his past,
        That he 's your fixed enemy, and revoke
        Your sudden approbation.
BRU.   Say, you ne'er had done 't—
        Harp on that still—but by our putting on: 260
        And presently, when you have drawn your number,
        Repair to the Capitol.
CITIZENS.   We will so: almost all
        Repent in their election.   [*Exeunt* Citizens.
BRU.   Let them go on;
        This mutiny were better put in hazard,
        Than stay, past doubt, for greater:
        If, as his nature is, he fall in rage
        With their refusal, both observe and answer
        The vantage of his anger.   270
SIC.   To the Capitol, come:
        We will be there before the stream o' the people;
        And this shall seem, as partly 't is, their own,
        Which we have goaded onward.   [*Exeunt*.

---

256 *Scaling*] Weighing, balancing.
260 *by our putting on*] at our instigation.
261 *drawn your number*] drawn together or levied the full number of your supporters.
269–270 *observe and answer . . . anger*] observe and be ready to take any advantage that
    his anger affords, improve the opportunity which his anger will offer.

ACT III.

SCENE I. *Rome. A Street.*

Cornets. Enter CORIOLANUS, MENENIUS, *all the* Gentry,
COMINIUS, TITUS LARTIUS, *and other* Senators

CORIOLANUS.   Tullus Aufidius then had made new head?
LART.   He had, my lord; and that it was which caused
    Our swifter composition.
COR.   So then the Volsces stand but as at first;
    Ready, when time shall prompt them, to make road
    Upon 's again.
COM.   They are worn, lord consul, so,
    That we shall hardly in our ages see
    Their banners wave again.
COR.   Saw you Aufidius?   10
LART.   On safe-guard he came to me; and did curse
    Against the Volsces, for they had so vilely
    Yielded the town: he is retired to Antium.
COR.   Spoke he of me?
LART.   He did, my lord.
COR.   How? what?
LART.   How often he had met you, sword to sword;
    That of all things upon the earth he hated
    Your person most; that he would pawn his fortunes
    To hopeless restitution, so he might   20
    Be call'd your vanquisher.
COR.   At Antium lives he?
LART.   At Antium.

---

1 *made new head*] raised a new body of troops.
 3 *Our swifter composition*] Our hurried negotiation of peace.
 5 *make road*] make advance.
11 *On safe-guard*] Under safe conduct, under escort.
20 *To hopeless restitution*] Without any hope of restitution.

COR.   I wish I had a cause to seek him there,
    To oppose his hatred fully. Welcome home.

Enter SICINIUS *and* BRUTUS

    Behold, these are the tribunes of the people,
    The tongues o' the common mouth: I do despise them;
    For they do prank them in authority,
    Against all noble sufferance.
SIC.   Pass no further.   30
COR.   Ha! what is that?
BRU.   It will be dangerous to go on: no further.
COR.   What makes this change?
MEN.   The matter?
COM.   Hath he not pass'd the noble and the common?
BRU.   Cominius, no.
COR.   Have I had children's voices?
FIRST SEN.   Tribunes, give way; he shall to the market-place.
BRU.   The people are incensed against him.
SIC.   Stop,   40
    Or all will fall in broil.
COR.   Are these your herd?
    Must these have voices, that can yield them now,
    And straight disclaim their tongues? What are your offices?
    You being their mouths, why rule you not their teeth?
    Have you not set them on?
MEN.   Be calm, be calm.
COR.   It is a purposed thing, and grows by plot,
    To curb the will of the nobility:
    Suffer 't, and live with such as cannot rule,   50
    Nor ever will be ruled.
BRU.   Call 't not a plot:
    The people cry you mock'd them; and of late,
    When corn was given them gratis, you repined,
    Scandal'd the suppliants for the people, call'd them
    Time-pleasers, flatterers, foes to nobleness.

---

28 *prank them*] plume themselves. Cf. *Meas for Meas.*, II, ii, 117–118: "man *Drest in* a
    little brief *authority*."
29 *Against all noble sufferance*] Past the endurance of all noble natures.
35 *noble . . . common*] Thus the First Folio. The later Folios read *noble . . . Commons*.
    Rowe adopted *nobles . . . commons*.
54 *you repined, Scandal'd*] you murmured against, you slandered. "Repine," which here
    seems to be used transitively, is commonly found as an intransitive verb (*i.e.*, "fret," or
    "murmur").

COR.   Why, this was known before.
BRU.   Not to them all.
COR.   Have you inform'd them sithence?
BRU.   How! I inform them!   60
COM.   You are like to do such business.
BRU.   Not unlike,
    Each way, to better yours.
COR.   Why then should I be consul? By yond clouds,
    Let me deserve so ill as you, and make me
    Your fellow tribune.
SIC.   You show too much of that
    For which the people stir: if you will pass
    To where you are bound, you must inquire your way,
    Which you are out of, with a gentler spirit;   70
    Or never be so noble as a consul,
    Nor yoke with him for tribune.
MEN.   Let 's be calm.
COM.   The people are abused; set on. This paltering
    Becomes not Rome; nor has Coriolanus
    Deserved this so dishonour'd rub, laid falsely
    I' the plain way of his merit.
COR.   Tell me of corn!
    This was my speech, and I will speak 't again—
MEN.   Not now, not now.   80
FIRST SEN.   Not in this heat, sir, now.
COR.   Now, as I live, I will. My nobler friends,
    I crave their pardons:
    For the mutable, rank-scented many, let them
    Regard me as I do not flatter, and
    Therein behold themselves: I say again,

59 *sithence*] an archaic form of "since."
61 *You are like . . . business*] The Folios assign this speech to Cominius, but Theobald reasonably transferred it to Coriolanus.
62–63 *Not unlike . . . yours*] We are not unlikely to take a better course than you in every direction.
74 *The people are abused; set on*] The people are deceived; let us get on with our business.
74 *paltering*] shuffling or haggling.
76 *dishonour'd rub*] dishonourable impediment; "rub" is the technical term for an obstacle in the way of a throw at the game of bowls.
76 *falsely*} treacherously.
84 *many*] the populace.
84–86 *let them . . . behold themselves*] let them turn their attention to me who am no flatterer of them, and see themselves in the mirror of my speech.

In soothing them, we nourish 'gainst our senate
The cockle of rebellion, insolence, sedition,
Which we ourselves have plough'd for, sow'd and scatter'd,
By mingling them with us, the honour'd number;   90
Who lack not virtue, no, nor power, but that
Which they have given to beggars.

MEN.   Well, no more.

FIRST SEN. No more words, we beseech you.

COR.   How! no more!
As for my country I have shed my blood,
Not fearing outward force, so shall my lungs
Coin words till their decay against those measles,
Which we disdain should tetter us, yet sought
The very way to catch them.   100

BRU.   You speak o' the people,
As if you were a god to punish, not
A man of their infirmity.

SIC.   'T were well
We let the people know 't.

MEN.   What, what? his choler?

COR. Choler!
Were I as patient as the midnight sleep,
By Jove, 't would be my mind!

SIC.   It is a mind   110
That shall remain a poison where it is,
Not poison any further.

COR.   Shall remain!
Hear you this Triton of the minnows? mark you
His absolute "shall"?

COM.   'T was from the canon.

COR.   "Shall"!

---

87 *soothing*] flattering.

88 *cockle*] a weed which poisons growing corn. Plutarch uses the word in the corresponding passage. Cf. *L. L. L.*, IV, iii, 379: "Sow'd *cockle* reap'd no corn."

98 *measles*] symptoms of leprosy; the disease now known as measles seems too mild for the context. "Mesell" a word of different derivation, with which "measles" might easily be confused, is often found in pre-Shakespearean literature alike for "leprous," "leper," and "leprosy."

99 *tetter us*] cover our skin with a scab. "Ringworm" is often called "tetter."

114 *Triton*] Properly a seagod, son to Neptune, whom he served as trumpeter. Ovid describes him in *Metam.*, I, 333. "The horn and noise o' the monster's," line 95, suggests some of his attributes.

116 *from the canon*] contrary to the law; an infringement of legal right.

O good, but most unwise patricians! why,
You grave but reckless senators, have you thus
Given Hydra here to choose an officer,   120
That with his peremptory "shall," being but
The horn and noise o' the monster's, wants not spirit
To say he'll turn your current in a ditch,
And make your channel his? If he have power,
Then vail your ignorance; if none, awake
Your dangerous lenity. If you are learn'd,
Be not as common fools; if you are not,
Let them have cushions by you. You are plebeians,
If they be senators: and they are no less,
When, both your voices blended, the great'st taste   130
Most palates theirs. They choose their magistrate;
And such a one as he, who puts his "shall,"
His popular "shall," against a graver bench
Than ever frown'd in Greece. By Jove himself,
It makes the consuls base! and my soul aches
To know, when two authorities are up,
Neither supreme, how soon confusion
May enter 'twixt the gap of both and take
The one by the other.
COM.   Well, on to the market-place.   140
COR.   Whoever gave that counsel, to give forth
The corn o' the storehouse gratis, as 't was used
Sometime in Greece,—
MEN.   Well, well, no more of that.
COR.   Though there the people had more absolute power,
I say, they nourish'd disobedience, fed
The ruin of the state.
BRU.   Why, shall the people give
One that speaks thus their voice?

---

118 *O good*] Pope's correction of the Folio reading *O God!*
120 *Hydra*] the many-headed monster, which is described by Ovid, *Metam.*, IX, 69, *seq.*
    Cf. IV, i, *infra*: "the beast With many heads," and 2 *Hen. IV, Induction*, 18.
122 *the monster's*] a reminiscence of the seagod Triton rather than of the many-headed
    Hydra; see l. 116, *supra*, and note.
125 *vail your ignorance*] lower, have done with your ignorance of, or indifference to, the
    power or pretension of the mob.
129–131 *they are no less . . . theirs*] The plebeians are no less than senators when both
    ranks are blended to an equality, and the predominant flavour of the mixture
    smacks most of the populace. In other words, if the upper and lower classes are to
    have an equal voice in affairs of state, the voice of the lower class will predominate.
136 *are up*] are in office.

COR.   I'll give my reasons,   150
    More worthier than their voices. They know the corn
    Was not our recompense, resting well assured
    They ne'er did service for 't: being press'd to the war,
    Even when the navel of the state was touch'd,
    They would not thread the gates. This kind of service
    Did not deserve corn gratis: being i' the war,
    Their mutinies and revolts, wherein they show'd
    Most valour, spoke not for them: the accusation
    Which they have often made against the senate,
    All cause unborn, could never be the native   160
    Of our so frank donation. Well, what then?
    How shall this bosom multiplied digest
    The senate's courtesy? Let deeds express
    What's like to be their words: "We did request it;
    We are the greater poll, and in true fear
    They gave us our demands." Thus we debase
    The nature of our seats, and make the rabble
    Call our cares fears; which will in time
    Break ope the locks o' the senate, and bring in
    The crows to peck the eagles.   170
MEN.   Come, enough.
BRU.   Enough, with over measure.
COR.   No, take more:
    What may be sworn by, both divine and human,
    Seal what I end withal! This double worship,
    Where one part does disdain with cause, the other
    Insult without all reason; where gentry, title, wisdom,
    Cannot conclude but by the yea and no
    Of general ignorance,—it must omit

152 *our recompense*] a reward given by us.
154 *when the navel . . . touch'd*] when the vital part of the state was menaced.
155 *thread*] pass through.
160 *All cause unborn*] With no shadow of justification.
160 *native*] origin, source. "Native" here means "natural parent" or "cause of birth."
    The usage is rare, though the word is frequently found for native place or country.
    Motive has been suggested in its stead.
162 *bosom multiplied*] multitudinous bosom, heart of the many-headed people.
163 *Let deeds . . . words*] Let their past acts indicate what they are likely to say.
165 *the greater poll*] the majority.
166–167 *debase . . . seats*] degrade the character of our position.
174–175 *What may be sworn by . . . withal*] May everything divine and human, which
    can give force to an oath, confirm the truth of my concluding words.
178 *conclude*] take a decision.
179 *general ignorance*] vulgar ignorance.

Real necessities, and give way the while   180
To unstable slightness: purpose so barr'd, it follows,
Nothing is done to purpose. Therefore, beseech you, —
You that will be less fearful than discreet;
That love the fundamental part of state
More than you doubt the change on 't; that prefer
A noble life before a long, and wish
To jump a body with a dangerous physic
That 's sure of death without it, — at once pluck out
The multitudinous tongue; let them not lick
The sweet which is their poison. Your dishonour   190
Mangles true judgement and bereaves the state
Of that integrity which should become 't;
Not having the power to do the good it would,
For the ill which doth control 't.

BRU.   Has said enough.
SIC.   Has spoken like a traitor, and shall answer
As traitors do.
COR.   Thou wretch, despite o'erwhelm thee!
What should the people do with these bald tribunes?
On whom depending, their obedience fails   200
To the greater bench: in a rebellion,
When what 's not meet, but what must be, was law,
Then were they chosen: in a better hour,
Let what is meet be said it must be meet,
And throw their power i' the dust.

BRU.   Manifest treason!
SIC.   This a consul? no.
BRU.   The ædiles, ho!

181–182 *purpose . . . purpose*] When the good design is so baulked, it follows that no
    useful act is performed. There is a slight quibble on two shades of meaning in the
    word "purpose."
184–185 *That love the fundamental part . . . change on 't*] You who have affection for
    the genuine interest of the state in larger measure than you have fear of the revo-
    lution (which may destroy the state).
187 *jump*] expose to hazard.
192 *integrity*] soundness.
198 *despite*] hate.
199 *bald*] paltry, witless. Cf. *1 Hen. IV*, I, iii, 65: "This *bald* unjointed chat."
201 *To the greater bench*] To magistrates in higher position.
204 *Let what . . . be meet*] Let it be said by you that what is meet to be done must be
    done.
208 *ædiles*] "ædiles plebeii," servants of the tribunes, who made arrests at their bidding and
    carried out death sentences. Of later date and higher rank were the "ædiles curules,"
    city officers who had control of the streets, buildings, games, baths, and the like.

Enter an Ædile

Let him be apprehended.

SIC.   Go, call the people: [*Exit* Ædile.] in whose name myself   210
    Attach thee as a traitorous innovator,
    A foe to the public weal: obey, I charge thee,
    And follow to thine answer.
COR.   Hence, old goat!
SENATORS, &C.   We'll surety him.
COM.   Aged sir, hands off.
COR.   Hence, rotten thing! or I shall shake thy bones
    Out of thy garments.
SIC.   Help, ye citizens!

Enter a rabble of Citizens, *with the* Ædiles

MEN.   On both sides more respect.   220
SIC.   Here 's he that would take from you all your power.
BRU.   Seize him, ædiles!
CITIZENS.   Down with him! down with him!
SENATORS, &C.   Weapons, weapons, weapons!
         [*They all bustle about* CORIOLANUS, *crying,*
    "Tribunes!" "Patricians!" "Citizens!" "What, ho!" "Sicinius!"
    "Brutus!" "Coriolanus!" "Citizens!" "Peace, peace, peace!"
    "Stay! hold! peace!"
MEN.   What is about to be? I am out of breath.
    Confusion's near. I cannot speak. You, tribunes
    To the people! Coriolanus, patience!   230
    Speak, good Sicinius.
SIC.   Hear me, people; peace!
CITIZENS.   Let's hear our tribune: peace!—Speak, speak, speak.
SIC.   You are at point to lose your liberties:
    Marcius would have all from you; Marcius,
    Whom late you have named for consul.
MEN.   Fie, fie, fie!
    This is the way to kindle, not to quench.
FIRST SEN.   To unbuild the city, and to lay all flat.
SIC.   What is the city but the people?   240
CITIZENS.   True,
    The people are the city.
BRU.   By the consent of all, we were establish'd
    The people's magistrates.

---

229 *You, tribunes*] The verb "speak" is obviously understood.
234 *at point*] on the point, about.

CITIZENS.   You so remain.
MEN.   And so are like to do.
COM.   That is the way to lay the city flat,
        To bring the roof to the foundation,
        And bury all which yet distinctly ranges,
        In heaps and piles of ruin.   250
SIC.   This deserves death.
BRU.   Or let us stand to our authority,
        Or let us lose it. We do here pronounce,
        Upon the part o' the people, in whose power
        We were elected theirs, Marcius is worthy
        Of present death.
SIC.   Therefore lay hold of him;
        Bear him to the rock Tarpeian, and from thence
        Into destruction cast him.
BRU.   Ædiles, seize him!   260
CITIZENS.   Yield, Marcius, yield!
MEN.   Hear me one word;
        Beseech you, tribunes, hear me but a word.
ÆDILES.   Peace, peace!
MEN. [*To* BRUTUS]   Be that you seem, truly your country's friend,
        And temperately proceed to what you would
        Thus violently redress.
BRU.   Sir, those cold ways,
        That seem like prudent helps, are very poisonous
        Where the disease is violent. Lay hands upon him,   270
        And bear him to the rock.
COR.   No, I'll die here.   [*Drawing his sword.*
        There's some among you have beheld me fighting:
        Come, try upon yourselves what you have seen me.
MEN.   Down with that sword! Tribunes, withdraw awhile.
BRU.   Lay hands upon him.
MEN.   Help Marcius, help,
        You that be noble; help him, young and old!
CITIZENS.   Down with him, down with him!

                    [*In this mutiny, the* Tribunes, *the* Ædiles,
                        and the People, *are beat in.*

249 *distinctly ranges*] is ranged in due order, is disposed in regular line or order.
258 *the rock Tarpeian*] the precipice on the Capitol whence criminals were flung and
    killed.
268 *those cold ways*] those dispassionate methods.

MEN.   Go, get you to your house; be gone, away!   280
      All will be naught else.
SEC. SEN.   Get you gone.
COM.   Stand fast;
      We have as many friends as enemies.
MEN.   Shall it be put to that?
FIRST SEN.   The gods forbid!
      I prithee, noble friend, home to thy house;
      Leave us to cure this cause.
MEN.   For 't is a sore upon us
      You cannot tent yourself: be gone, beseech you.   290
COM.   Come, sir, along with us.
COR.   I would they were barbarians—as they are,
      Though in Rome litter'd—not Romans—as they are not,
      Though calved i' the porch o' the Capitol,—
MEN.   Be gone:
      Put not your worthy rage into your tongue:
      One time will owe another.
COR.   On fair ground
      I could beat forty of them.
MEN.   I could myself   300
      Take up a brace o' the best of them; yea, the two tribunes.
COM.   But now 't is odds beyond arithmetic;
      And manhood is call'd foolery, when it stands
      Against a falling fabric. Will you hence
      Before the tag return? whose rage doth rend
      Like interrupted waters, and o'erbear
      What they are used to bear.
MEN.   Pray you, be gone:
      I'll try whether my old wit be in request
      With those that have but little: this must be patch'd   310
      With cloth of any colour.

---

290 *tent*] probe with a view to curing; a familiar term in surgery.
295–297 *Be gone . . . owe another*] The Folios make these words part of Coriolanus' pre-
      ceding speech. Steevens seems to have first assigned them to "Menenius," to whom
      they are clearly appropriate.
297 *One time . . . another*] One time will compensate for another; our time of triumph
      is coming.
302 *beyond arithmetic*] past calculation.
305 *the tag*] the rabble; commonly associated with the phrase "tag, rag and bobtail." Cf.
      Jul. Cæs., I, ii, 255: "the *tag rag* people."
306 *Like interrupted waters . . . bear*] Like waters whose flow is forcibly obstructed, so
      that in the overflow they overwhelm whatever is on their surface. Cf. *Two Gent.*, II,
      vii, 25–26: "The current . . . being stopp'd, impatiently doth rage."

COM.   Nay, come away.

[*Exeunt* CORIOLANUS, COMINIUS, *and others*.

FIRST PATRICIAN.   This man has marr'd his fortune.
MEN.   His nature is too noble for the world:
    He would not flatter Neptune for his trident,
    Or Jove for 's power to thunder. His heart 's his mouth:
    What his breast forges, that his tongue must vent;
    And, being angry, does forget that ever
    He heard the name of death.   [*A noise within*.
    Here 's goodly work!   320
SEC. PAT.   I would they were a-bed!
MEN.   I would they were in Tiber! What, the vengeance,
    Could he not speak 'em fair?

Re-enter BRUTUS *and* SICINIUS, *with the rabble*

SIC.   Where is this viper,
    That would depopulate the city, and
    Be every man himself?
MEN.   You worthy tribunes—
SIC.   He shall be thrown down the Tarpeian rock
    With rigorous hands: he hath resisted law,
    And therefore law shall scorn him further trial   330
    Than the severity of the public power,
    Which he so sets at nought.
FIRST CIT.   He shall well know
    The noble tribunes are the people's mouths,
    And we their hands.
CITIZENS.   He shall, sure on 't.
MEN.   Sir, sir,—
SIC.   Peace!
MEN.   Do not cry havoc, where you should but hunt
    With modest warrant.   340
SIC.   Sir, how comes 't that you
    Have holp to make this rescue?
MEN.   Hear me speak:
    As I do know the consul's worthiness,
    So can I name his faults,—

339 *cry havoc*] cry the signal for "no quarter," for indiscriminate slaughter. Cf. *Jul. Cæs.*,
    III, i, 274: "*Cry havoc*, and let slip the dogs of war." "Havoc" seems to represent an
    ancient form of "hawk," and the phrase seems to have originated among those en-
    gaged in the sport of falconry.

SIC.   Consul! what consul?
MEN.   The consul Coriolanus.
BRU.   He consul!
CITIZENS.   No, no, no, no, no.
MEN.   If, by the tribunes' leave, and yours, good people,   350
     I may be heard, I would crave a word or two;
     The which shall turn you to no further harm
     Than so much loss of time.
SIC.   Speak briefly then;
     For we are peremptory to dispatch
     This viperous traitor: to eject him hence
     Were but one danger, and to keep him here
     Our certain death: therefore it is decreed
     He dies to-night.
MEN.   Now the good gods forbid   360
     That our renowned Rome, whose gratitude
     Towards her deserved children is enroll'd
     In Jove's own book, like an unnatural dam
     Should now eat up her own!
SIC.   He 's a disease that must be cut away.
MEN.   O, he 's a limb that has but a disease;
     Mortal, to cut it off; cure it, easy.
     What has he done to Rome that 's worthy death?
     Killing our enemies, the blood he hath lost—
     Which, I dare vouch, is more than that he hath   370
     By many an ounce—he dropp'd it for his country;
     And what is left, to lose it by his country
     Were to us all that do 't and suffer it
     A brand to the end o' the world.
SIC.   This is clean kam.
BRU.   Merely awry: when he did love his country,
     It honour'd him.

352 *turn you to*] expose you to.
357 *one*] complete, whole. Thus the Folios; Theobald substituted *our*.
362 *deserved*] deserving.
367 *Mortal*] Fatal, deadly.
374 *brand*] sc. of infamy.
375 *clean kam*] These words are synonymous with "merely (*i.e.*, absolutely) awry" which
     immediately follow them. "Kam" is an old Celtic word for "crooked," which sur-
     vives in the river-name Cam in Cambridge.

MEN.   The service of the foot
  Being once gangrened, is not then respected
  For what before it was.   380
BRU.   We 'll hear no more.
  Pursue him to his house, and pluck him thence;
  Lest his infection, being of catching nature,
  Spread further.
MEN.   One word more, one word.
  This tiger-footed rage, when it shall find
  The harm of unscann'd swiftness, will, too late,
  Tie leaden pounds to 's heels. Proceed by process;
  Lest parties, as he is beloved, break out,
  And sack great Rome with Romans.   390
BRU.   If it were so —
SIC. What do ye talk?
  Have we not had a taste of his obedience?
  Our ædiles smote? ourselves resisted? Come.
MEN. Consider this: he has been bred i' the wars
  Since he could draw a sword, and is ill school'd
  In bolted language; meal and bran together
  He throws without distinction. Give me leave,
  I'll go to him, and undertake to bring him
  Where he shall answer, by a lawful form,   400
  In peace, to his utmost peril.
FIRST SEN.   Noble tribunes,
  It is the humane way: the other course
  Will prove too bloody; and the end of it
  Unknown to the beginning.
SIC.   Noble Menenius,
  Be you then as the people's officer.
  Masters, lay down your weapons.
BRU.   Go not home.
SIC. Meet on the market-place. We'll attend you there: 410
  Where, if you bring not Marcius, we'll proceed
  In our first way.
MEN.   I'll bring him to you.

---

378 *The service of the foot . . . before it was*] Menenius is here ironically adopting the tribune's own line of argument, doubtless with a view to reducing it to absurdity, when he is interrupted by the impatient Brutus. Hanmer would give the speech to the tribune Sicinius; others would make it part of Brutus' preceding remark.
387 *unscann'd swiftness*] inconsiderate or rash haste.
397 *bolted*] refined, sifted.

[*To the* Senators] Let me desire your company: he must
    come,
Or what is worst will follow.
FIRST SEN.   Pray you, let's to him.   [*Exeunt.*

SCENE II. *A Room in Coriolanus's House.*

Enter CORIOLANUS *with* Patricians

COR.   Let them pull all about mine ears; present me
    Death on the wheel, or at wild horses' heels;
    Or pile ten hills on the Tarpeian rock,
    That the precipitation might down stretch
    Below the beam of sight; yet will I still
    Be thus to them.
A PATRICIAN.   You do the nobler.
COR.   I muse my mother
    Does not approve me further, who was wont
    To call them woollen vassals, things created   10
    To buy and sell with groats, to show bare heads
    In congregations, to yawn, be still and wonder,
    When one but of my ordinance stood up
    To speak of peace or war.

Enter VOLUMNIA

                     I talk of you:
    Why did you wish me milder? would you have me
    False to my nature? Rather say, I play
    The man I am.
VOL.   O, sir, sir, sir,
    I would have had you put your power well on,   20
    Before you had worn it out.
COR.   Let go.
VOL.   You might have been enough the man you are,
    With striving less to be so: lesser had been
    The thwartings of your dispositions, if

---

5 *beam of sight*] ray of sight, range of vision.
8 *muse*] wonder.
10 *woollen vassals*] coarse-clothed fellows. Cf. *Mids. N. Dr.*, III, i, 68: "hempen home-
    spuns."
13 *ordinance*] order, rank.
25 *thwartings of your dispositions*] Theobald's correction of the Folio reading *things of
    your dispositions.*

You had not show'd them how ye were disposed,
Ere they lack'd power to cross you.

COR.   Let them hang.

VOL. Ay, and burn too.

Enter MENENIUS *with the* Senators

MEN. Come, come, you have been too rough, something too
  rough;   30
  You must return and mend it.

FIRST SEN.   There 's no remedy;
  Unless, by not so doing, our good city
  Cleave in the midst, and perish.

VOL.   Pray, be counsell'd:
  I have a heart as little apt as yours,
  But yet a brain that leads my use of anger
  To better vantage.

MEN.   Well said, noble woman!
  Before he should thus stoop to the herd, but that   40
  The violent fit o' the time craves it as physic
  For the whole state, I would put mine armour on,
  Which I can scarcely bear.

COR.   What must I do?

MEN. Return to the tribunes.

COR.   Well, what then? what then?

MEN. Repent what you have spoke.

COR. For them! I cannot do it to the gods;
  Must I then do 't to them?

VOL.   You are too absolute;   50
  Though therein you can never be too noble,
  But when extremities speak. I have heard you say,
  Honour and policy, like unsever'd friends,
  I' the war do grow together: grant that, and tell me,
  In peace what each of them by the other lose,
  That they combine not there.

---

28 *Ay, and burn too*] This is an involuntary outburst of Volumnia's horror of the mob.
 Some editors object needlessly that the words are inconsistent with the speaker's plea
 for patience.

36 *apt*] *sc.* to submit, submissive. Thus the Folios. Many changes have been suggested.
 But though the expression is elliptical, the context makes the meaning plain.

40 *the herd*] Theobald's correction of the Folio reading *th' heart*. Coriolanus has twice
 already applied the word "herd" to the rabble of Rome, I, iv, 36, and III, i, 42, *supra*.

50–52 *You are too absolute . . . extremities speak*] You are too self-confident; your resolution and self-confidence can never be out of place in a noble heart, except in the
 presence of desperate dangers.

COR.   Tush, tush!
MEN.   A good demand.
VOL.   If it be honour in your wars to seem
    The same you are not, which, for your best ends,   60
    You adopt your policy, how is it less or worse,
    That it shall hold companionship in peace
    With honour, as in war, since that to both
    It stands in like request?
COR.   Why force you this?
VOL.   Because that now it lies you on to speak
    To the people; not by your own instruction,
    Nor by the matter which your heart prompts you,
    But with such words that are but roted in
    Your tongue, though but bastards and syllables   70
    Of no allowance to your bosom's truth.
    Now, this no more dishonours you at all
    Than to take in a town with gentle words,
    Which else would put you to your fortune and
    The hazard of much blood.
    I would dissemble with my nature, where
    My fortunes and my friends at stake required
    I should do so in honour. I am in this,
    Your wife, your son, these senators, the nobles;
    And you will rather show our general louts   80
    How you can frown than spend a fawn upon 'em,
    For the inheritance of their love and safeguard
    Of what that want might ruin.
MEN.   Noble lady!
    Come, go with us; speak fair: you may salve so,
    Not what is dangerous present, but the loss
    Of what is past.
VOL.   I prithee now, my son,
    Go to them, with this bonnet in thy hand;

---

65 *force*] press, urge.
69–70 *roted in Your tongue*] learnt by rote, not uttered spontaneously.
71 *Of no allowance . . . truth*] Without the authority or approbation of the truth which
    is innate in your heart.
73 *take in*] conquer, subdue. Cf. I, ii, 27, *supra*.
74 *put you to your fortune*] make you risk or imperil your fortune.
78–79 *I am in this . . . nobles*] I am spokesman in this matter for your wife, etc.
80 *our general louts*] our common people.
83 *that want*] the want of their love, their enmity.
86 *Not what is*] Not only, not merely, what is.
89 *this bonnet*] Volumnia points to Coriolanus' head-gear.

And thus far having stretch'd it—here be with them—   90
Thy knee bussing the stones—for in such business
Action is eloquence, and the eyes of the ignorant
More learned than the ears—waving thy head,
Which often, thus, correcting thy stout heart,
Now humble as the ripest mulberry
That will not hold the handling: or say to them,
Thou art their soldier, and being bred in broils
Hast not the soft way which, thou dost confess,
Were fit for thee to use, as they to claim,
In asking their good loves; but thou wilt frame   100
Thyself, forsooth, hereafter theirs, so far
As thou hast power and person.

MEN.   This but done,
Even as she speaks, why, their hearts were yours;
For they have pardons, being ask'd, as free
As words to little purpose.

VOL.   Prithee now,
Go, and be ruled: although I know thou hadst rather
Follow thine enemy in a fiery gulf
Than flatter him in a bower.   110

Enter COMINIUS

                   Here is Cominius.
COM.   I have been i' the market-place; and, sir, 't is fit
You make strong party, or defend yourself
By calmness or by absence: all 's in anger.
MEN.   Only fair speech.
COM.   I think 't will serve, if he
Can thereto frame his spirit.
VOL.   He must, and will.
Prithee now, say you will, and go about it.

90 *here be with them*] here set yourself on a level with them, show them deference.
91 *bussing*] kissing.
93 *waving*] gently moving or bowing.
94 *Which often, thus,*] This is the punctuation of the Folios, and is difficult. Only one comma is required, and should follow *which*.
95 *humble*] This word is here the imperative of the verb "to humble," and governs as its object "Which" (*i.e.*, the head), in the previous line.
95–96 *the ripest mulberry . . . handling*] The fully-ripe mulberry is detached from the tree at the slightest touch of the hand.
102 *power and person*] individual or personal capacity.
105 *they have pardons . . . little purpose*] they are prone to grant pardon when asked as readily as to speak words of no particular significance.
113 *You make strong party*] You collect a strong body of supporters.

Cor.   Must I go show them my unbarb'd sconce? must I,   120
          With my base tongue, give to my noble heart
          A lie, that it must bear? Well, I will do 't:
          Yet, were there but this single plot to lose,
          This mould of Marcius, they to dust should grind it,
          And throw 't against the wind. To the market-place!
          You have put me now to such a part, which never
          I shall discharge to the life.
Com.   Come, come, we 'll prompt you.
Vol.   I prithee now, sweet son, as thou hast said
          My praises made thee first a soldier, so,   130
          To have my praise for this, perform a part
          Thou hast not done before.
Cor.   Well, I must do 't:
          Away, my disposition, and possess me
          Some harlot's spirit! my throat of war be turn'd,
          Which quired with my drum, into a pipe
          Small as an eunuch, or the virgin voice
          That babies lulls asleep! the smiles of knaves
          Tent in my cheeks, and schoolboys' tears take up
          The glasses of my sight! a beggar's tongue   140
          Make motion through my lips, and my arm'd knees,
          Who bow'd but in my stirrup, bend like his
          That hath received an alms! I will not do 't;
          Lest I surcease to honour mine own truth,
          And by my body's action teach my mind
          A most inherent baseness.
Vol.   At thy choice then:
          To beg of thee, it is my more dishonour
          Than thou of them. Come all to ruin: let
          Thy mother rather feel thy pride than fear   150
          Thy dangerous stoutness, for I mock at death
          With as big heart as thou. Do as thou list.

---

120 *unbarb'd sconce*] uncovered head. "Barbed" (or "barded") is often found in the sense
      of "armoured" or "covered with armour." Cf. *Rich. III*, I, i, 10: "*barbed* steeds."
123 *this single plot*] this sole piece of earth, my own mere body only.
135 *some harlot's spirit*] Some ribald's spirit. "Harlot" as a term of contempt was applied
      to men as well as to women.
136 *quired*] played in concert.
139 *Tent in . . . take up*] encamp, lodge in . . . occupy.
144 *surcease to honour*] cease to honour, give over respecting.
149–151 *let Thy mother . . . stoutness*] let thy mother rather suffer the worst from thy
      pride than continue to live in nervous fear of thy dangerous obstinacy. Volumnia
      deprecates the uncertainty of the issue.

Thy valiantness was mine, thou suck'dst it from me,
But owe thy pride thyself.
COR.   Pray, be content:
  Mother, I am going to the market-place;
  Chide me no more. I'll mountebank their loves,
  Cog their hearts from them, and come home beloved
  Of all the trades in Rome. Look, I am going:
  Commend me to my wife. I'll return consul;   160
  Or never trust to what my tongue can do
  I' the way of flattery further.
VOL.   Do your will.   [*Exit.*
COM.   Away! the tribunes do attend you: arm yourself
  To answer mildly; for they are prepared
  With accusations, as I hear, more strong
  Than are upon you yet.
COR.   The word is "mildly." Pray you, let us go:
  Let them accuse me by invention, I
  Will answer in mine honour.   170
MEN.   Ay, but mildly.
COR.   Well, mildly be it then. Mildly!   [*Exeunt.*

SCENE III. *The Same. The Forum.*

Enter SICINIUS *and* BRUTUS

BRU.   In this point charge him home, that he affects
  Tyrannical power: if he evade us there,
  Enforce him with his envy to the people;
  And that the spoil got on the Antiates
  Was ne'er distributed.

Enter an Ædile

  What, will he come?
ÆD.   He 's coming.
BRU.   How accompanied?
ÆD.   With old Menenius and those senators
  That always favour'd him.   10

---

154 *owe*] own.
157 *I'll mountebank their loves*] I'll play the conjurer and thereby get their loves.
158 *Cog*] Get by cheating.

3 *enforce him with his envy*] Press him hard with, urge against him, his hatred. Cf. II,
  iii, 223, *supra*: "*Enforce* his pride."

Sic.   Have you a catalogue
    Of all the voices that we have procured,
    Set down by the poll?
Æd.   I have; 't is ready.
Sic. Have you collected them by tribes?
Æd.   I have.
Sic. Assemble presently the people hither:
    And when they hear me say "It shall be so
    I' the right and strength o' the commons," be it either
    For death, for fine, or banishment, then let them,   20
    If I say fine, cry "Fine," if death, cry "Death,"
    Insisting on the old prerogative
    And power i' the truth o' the cause.
Æd.   I shall inform them.
Bru. And when such time they have begun to cry,
    Let them not cease, but with a din confused
    Enforce the present execution
    Of what we chance to sentence.
Æd.   Very well,
Sic. Make them be strong, and ready for this hint,   30
    When we shall hap to give 't them.
Bru.   Go about it.
                          [*Exit* Ædile.
    Put him to choler straight: he hath been used
    Ever to conquer and to have his worth
    Of contradiction: being once chafed, he cannot
    Be rein'd again to temperance; then he speaks
    What 's in his heart; and that is there which looks
    With us to break his neck.
Sic.   Well, here he comes.

Enter Coriolanus, Menenius, *and* Cominius, *with* Senators
    and Patricians

Men. Calmly, I do beseech you.   40
Cor. Ay, as an ostler, that for the poorest piece
    Will bear the knave by the volume. The honour'd gods
    Keep Rome in safety, and the chairs of justice
    Supplied with worthy men! plant love among 's!

34–35 *have his worth Of contradiction*] gain what he thinks worth disputing about.
37–38 *which looks With us*] which seems likely with our aid.
41 *for the poorest piece . . . volume*] for the smallest coin will stand being called knave
    often enough to fill a volume.

Throng our large temples with the shows of peace,
And not our streets with war!
FIRST SEN.   Amen, amen.
MEN.   A noble wish.

Re-enter Ædile, with Citizens

SIC.   Draw near, ye people.
ÆD.   List to your tribunes; audience: peace, I say!   50
COR.   First, hear me speak.
BOTH TRI.   Well, say. Peace, ho!
COR.   Shall I be charged no further than this present?
        Must all determine here?
SIC.   I do demand,
        If you submit you to the people's voices,
        Allow their officers, and are content
        To suffer lawful censure for such faults
        As shall be proved upon you.
COR.   I am content.   60
MEN.   Lo, citizens, he says he is content:
        The warlike service he has done, consider; think
        Upon the wounds his body bears, which show
        Like graves i' the holy churchyard.
COR.   Scratches with briers,
        Scars to move laughter only.
MEN.   Consider further,
        That when he speaks not like a citizen,
        You find him like a soldier: do not take
        His rougher accents for malicious sounds,   70
        But, as I say, such as become a soldier
        Rather than envy you.
COM.   Well, well, no more.
COR.   What is the matter
        That being pass'd for consul with full voice
        I am so dishonour'd that the very hour
        You take it off again?
SIC.   Answer to us.
COR.   Say, then: 't is true, I ought so.
SIC.   We charge you, that you have contrived to take   80

45 *Throng*] Theobald's correction of the Folio misreading *Through*.
45 *shows*] emblems.
70 *accents*] Theobald's corrections of the Folio misreading *Actions*.
72 *envy you*] malign or spite you.
80 *contrived*] planned, plotted.

From Rome a season'd office, and to wind
Yourself into a power tyrannical;
For which you are a traitor to the people.
COR.   How! traitor!
MEN.   Nay, temperately; your promise.
COR.   The fires i' the lowest hell fold-in the people!
Call me their traitor! Thou injurious tribune!
Within thine eyes sat twenty thousand deaths,
In thy hands clutch'd as many millions, in
Thy lying tongue both numbers, I would say   90
"Thou liest" unto thee with a voice as free
As I do pray the gods.
SIC.   Mark you this, people?
CITIZENS.   To the rock, to the rock with him!
SIC.   Peace!
We need not put new matter to his charge:
What you have seen him do and heard him speak,
Beating your officers, cursing yourselves,
Opposing laws with strokes, and here defying
Those whose great power must try him; even this,   100
So criminal and in such capital kind,
Deserves the extremest death.
BRU.   But since he hath
Served well for Rome—
COR.   What do you prate of service?
BRU.   I talk of that, that know it.
COR.   You?
MEN.   Is this the promise that you made your mother?
COM.   Know, I pray you,—
COR.   I'll know no further: 110
Let them pronounce the steep Tarpeian death,
Vagabond exile, flaying, pent to linger
But with a grain a day, I would not buy
Their mercy at the price of one fair word,
Nor check my courage for what they can give,
To have 't with saying "Good morrow."
SIC.   For that he has,
As much as in him lies, from time to time
Envied against the people, seeking means

81 *season'd*] established by time and custom.
87 *injurious*] insolent, insulting.
89 *In thy hands clutch'd*] Were there clutched or grasped in thy hands.
119 *Envied against*] Maligned, expressed himself with malice against.

To pluck away their power, as now at last   120
Given hostile strokes, and that not in the presence
Of dreaded justice, but on the ministers
That do distribute it; in the name o' the people,
And in the power of us the tribunes, we,
Even from this instant, banish him our city,
In peril of precipitation
From off the rock Tarpeian, never more
To enter our Rome gates: i' the people's name,
I say it shall be so.
CITIZENS.   It shall be so, it shall be so; let him away: 130
He 's banish'd, and it shall be so.
COM.   Hear me, my masters, and my common friends,—
SIC.   He 's sentenced; no more hearing.
COM.   Let me speak:
I have been consul, and can show for Rome
Her enemies' marks upon me. I do love
My country's good with a respect more tender,
More holy and profound, than mine own life,
My dear wife's estimate, her womb's increase
And treasure of my loins; then if I would   140
Speak that—
SIC.   We know your drift:—speak what?
BRU.   There 's no more to be said, but he is banish'd,
As enemy to the people and his country:
It shall be so.
CITIZENS.   It shall be so, it shall be so.
COR.   You common cry of curs! whose breath I hate
As reek o' the rotten fens, whose loves I prize
As the dead carcasses of unburied men
That do corrupt my air, I banish you;   150
And here remain with your uncertainty!
Let every feeble rumour shake your hearts!
Your enemies, with nodding of their plumes,
Fan you into despair! Have the power still
To banish your defenders; till at length

---

121 *not*] not only, not merely. Cf. III, ii, 86, *supra*.
135 *for Rome*] Theobald's correction for the Folio *from Rome*. Cf. IV, ii, 38, *infra*: "good
    man, the wounds that he does bear *for Rome*."
139 *estimate*] reputation.
147 *common cry*] vulgar pack. Cf. IV, vi, 182, *infra*: "you and *your cry*."
148 *As reek . . . rotten fens*] Cf. *Tempest*, II, i, 45–46: "As if it had lungs, and rotten ones.
    Or as 't were perfumed by a fen."

Your ignorance, which finds not till it feels,
Making not reservation of yourselves,
Still your own foes, deliver you as most
Abated captives to some nation
That won you without blows! Despising,   160
For you, the city, thus I turn my back:
There is a world elsewhere.

[*Exeunt* Coriolanus, Cominius, Menenius,
                    Senators *and* Patricians.

Æd.   The people's enemy is gone, is gone!
Citizens.   Our enemy is banish'd! he is gone! Hoo! hoo!
                    [*They all shout, and throw up their caps.*
Sic.   Go, see him out at gates, and follow him,
As he hath follow'd you, with all despite;
Give him deserved vexation. Let a guard
Attend us through the city.
Citizens.   Come, come, let's see him out at gates; come.
The gods preserve our noble tribunes! Come.   [*Exeunt.*   170

---

156 *which finds not till it feels*] Cf. the familiar political maxim in James Harrington's
    Oceana, 1656: "The people cannot see but they can feel."
157 *Making not reservation of yourselves*] Making no attempt to reserve or preserve the
    means of defending yourselves. *Not* is Capell's substitution for the Folio reading
    but, which would give the line the different and less coherent sense of "only work-
    ing in order to preserve your mere lives in the city."
159 *Abated*] Dejected, depressed.

ACT IV.

SCENE I. *Rome. Before a Gate of the City.*

Enter CORIOLANUS, VOLUMNIA, VIRGILIA, MENENIUS, COMINIUS,
with the young Nobility of Rome

CORIOLANUS.   Come, leave your tears; a brief farewell: the beast
    With many heads butts me away. Nay, mother,
    Where is your ancient courage? you were used
    To say extremity was the trier of spirits;
    That common chances common men could bear;
    That when the sea was calm all boats alike
    Show'd mastership in floating; fortune's blows,
    When most struck home, being gentle wounded, craves
    A noble cunning: you were used to load me
    With precepts that would make invincible   10
    The heart that conn'd them.
VIR.   O heavens! O heavens!
COR.   Nay, I prithee, woman,—
VOL.   Now the red pestilence strike all trades in Rome,
    And occupations perish!
COR.   What, what, what!

---

1 *the beast With many heads*] Cf. III, i, 120, *supra,* and 2 *Hen. IV, Induction,* 18: "the
    blunt *monster with uncounted heads.*"
4 *extremity*] desperate misfortune. Thus the Second and later Folios. The First Folio
    gives the word in the plural.
6–7 *when the sea . . . floating*] The same illustration is employed in *Troil. and Cress.,*
    I, iii, 33–37.
7–9 *fortune's blows . . . cunning*] when Fortune strikes her hardest blows, it requires a
    noble wisdom to suffer the wounds with gentle resignation. The language is harsh
    and elliptical, but the sense is clear. Thus the First Folio. None of the suggested
    emendations merits attention.
14 *the red pestilence*] Cf. *Tempest,* I, ii, 364: "The *red plague* rid you."
15 *occupations*] trades, callings, employment. Cf. IV, vi, 122, *infra:* "the voice of *occupation*" (*i.e.,* the working class), and *Tempest,* II, i, 148: "No *occupation*; all men idle."

I shall be loved when I am lack'd. Nay, mother,
Resume that spirit when you were wont to say,
If you had been the wife of Hercules,
Six of his labours you 'ld have done, and saved   20
Your husband so much sweat. Cominius,
Droop not; adieu. Farewell, my wife, my mother:
I'll do well yet. Thou old and true Menenius,
Thy tears are salter than a younger man's,
And venomous to thine eyes. My sometime general
I have seen thee stern, and thou hast oft beheld
Heart-hardening spectacles; tell these sad women,
'T is fond to wail inevitable strokes,
As 't is to laugh at 'em. My mother, you wot well
My hazards still have been your solace: and   30
Believe 't not lightly—though I go alone,
Like to a lonely dragon, that his fen
Makes fear'd and talk'd of more than seen—your son
Will or exceed the common, or be caught
With cautelous baits and practice.

VOL.   My first son,
Whither wilt thou go? Take good Cominius
With thee awhile: determine on some course,
More than a wild exposture to each chance
That starts i' the way before thee.   40

COR.   O the gods!

COM.   I'll follow thee a month, devise with thee
Where thou shalt rest, that thou mayst hear of us
And we of thee: so, if the time thrust forth
A cause for thy repeal, we shall not send
O'er the vast world to seek a single man,
And lose advantage, which doth ever cool
I' the absence of the needer.

COR.   Fare ye well:
Thou hast years upon thee; and thou art too full   50
Of the wars' surfeits, to go rove with one
That's yet unbruised: bring me but out at gate.

---

28 *fond*] foolish.

34 *or exceed the common*] either surpass or outdo the ordinary exploits (such as have formerly been his mother's consolation).

35 *cautelous*] crafty, dishonest.

35 *practice*] trick or stratagem.

39 *exposture*] an unusual form of "exposure." Cf. *Tim. of Ath.*, IV, iii, 439: "composture." The similar form "imposture" is in common use.

51 *the wars' surfeits*] excesses of war, the rough usages of war.

  Come, my sweet wife, my dearest mother, and
  My friends of noble touch, when I am forth,
  Bid me farewell, and smile. I pray you, come.
  While I remain above the ground, you shall
  Hear from me still, and never of me aught
  But what is like me formerly.
MEN.   That 's worthily
  As any ear can hear. Come, let 's not weep.   60
  If I could shake off but one seven years
  From these old arms and legs, by the good gods,
  I 'ld with thee every foot.
COR.   Give me thy hand:
  Come.   [*Exeunt.*

SCENE II. *The Same. A Street near the Gate.*

Enter the two Tribunes, SICINIUS, *and* BRUTUS, *with the* Ædile

SIC. Bid them all home; he's gone, and we'll no further.
  The nobility are vex'd, whom we see have sided
  In his behalf.
BRU.   Now we have shown our power,
  Let us seem humbler after it is done
  Than when it was a-doing.
SIC.   Bid them home:
  Say their great enemy is gone, and they
  Stand in their ancient strength.
BRU.   Dismiss them home.   10
          [*Exit* Ædile.
  Here comes his mother.

Enter VOLUMNIA, VIRGILIA, *and* MENENIUS

SIC.   Let 's not meet her.
BRU.   Why?
SIC. They say she 's mad.
BRU. They have ta'en note of us: keep on your way:
VOL. O, ye're well met: the hoarded plague o' the gods
  Requite your love!

---

54 *of noble touch*] of true metal; an allusion to the touchstone, whereby metals are tested. Cf. *Tim. of Ath.*, IV, iii, 387, where gold is called the "*touch* of hearts."

---

16 *the hoarded plague . . . your love!*] Cf. *Lear*, II, iv, 160–161: "All the *stored vengeances of heaven* fall On her ungrateful top."

MEN.	Peace, peace; be not so loud.
VOL.	If that I could for weeping, you should hear,—

Nay, and you shall hear some. [*To* BRUTUS] Will you be   20
    gone?

VIR. [*To* SICINIUS]   You shall stay too: I would I had the power
    To say so to my husband.

SIC.   Are you mankind?

VOL.   Ay, fool; is that a shame? Note but this fool.
    Was not a man my father? Hadst thou foxship
    To banish him that struck more blows for Rome
    Than thou hast spoken words?

SIC.   O blessed heavens!

VOL.   Moe noble blows than ever thou wise words;
    And for Rome's good. I'll tell thee what; yet go: 30
    Nay, but thou shalt stay too: I would my son
    Were in Arabia, and thy tribe before him,
    His good sword in his hand.

SIC.   What then?

VIR.   What then!
    He'ld make an end of thy posterity.

VOL.   Bastards and all.
    Good man, the wounds that he does bear for Rome!

MEN.   Come, come, peace.

SIC.   I would he had continued to his country   40
    As he began, and not unknit himself
    The noble knot he made.

BRU.   I would he had.

VOL.   "I would he had!" 'T was you incensed the rabble;
    Cats, that can judge as fitly of his worth

24–25 *Are you mankind? . . . shame?*] "Mankind" is first used in the sense of "man," "masculine creature lacking feminine gentleness." Cf. *Wint. Tale*, II, iii, 67: "A *mankind witch!*" Volumnia in her retort credits the word with the more general meaning of a "human being."

25 *foxship*] the mean cunning of an ungrateful fox. The form seems unknown elsewhere, though "foxy" in the sense of "crafty" is not uncommon. Foxes were held to be typical of ingratitude. Cf. *Lear*, III, vii, 28: "Ingrateful fox!"

31–32 *I would my son Were in Arabia*] Arabia is used generally of a desert country. Cf. *Cymb.*, I, i, 167: "I would they were in *Afric*," and *Macb.*, III, iv, 104: "dare me to the desert with thy sword."

38 *Good man . . . for Rome!*] Cf. III, iii, 135, *supra*.

41 *unknit himself*] himself untied. Cf. *1 Hen. IV*, V, i, 15–16: "will you again *unknit* This churlish *knot?*"

45 *Cats*] This word of reproach, which Volumnia addresses to the tribunes, was a common term of reproach. Cf. *All's Well*, IV, iii, 222: "now he's *a cat* to me."

As I can of those mysteries which heaven
Will not have earth to know.

BRU.　　　　　　　　　　　Pray, let us go.

VOL.　Now, pray, sir, get you gone:
You have done a brave deed. Ere you go, hear this:　　　　50
As far as doth the Capitol exceed
The meanest house in Rome, so far my son—
This lady's husband here, this, do you see?—
Whom you have banish'd, does exceed you all.

BRU.　Well, well, we'll leave you.

SIC.　　　　　　　　　　　Why stay we to be baited
With one that wants her wits?

VOL.　　　　　　　　　　Take my prayers with you.
　　　　　　　　　　　　　　　[*Exeunt* Tribunes.
I would the gods had nothing else to do
But to confirm my curses! Could I meet 'em　　　　60
But once a-day, it would unclog my heart
Of what lies heavy to 't.

MEN.　　　　　　　　You have told them home;
And, by my troth, you have cause. You'll sup with me?

VOL.　Anger's my meat; I sup upon myself,
And so shall starve with feeding. Come, let 's go:
Leave this faint puling, and lament as I do,
In anger, Juno-like. Come, come, come.
　　　　　　　　　　　　[*Exeunt* VOL. *and* VIR.

MEN.　Fie, fie, fie!　　　　　　　　　　　[*Exit.

SCENE III. A *Highway between Rome and Antium.*

Enter a Roman *and a* Volsce, *meeting*

ROM.　I know you well, sir, and you know me: your name, I
　think, is Adrian.

VOLS.　It is so, sir: truly, I have forgot you.

ROM.　I am a Roman; and my services are, as you are, against
　'em: know you me yet?

56–57 *baited With one*] teased or taunted by one.
60 *confirm*] ratify, put into effect.
60 *meet 'em*] meet the tribunes.
63 *You have told them home*] You have spoken out plainly: you have driven your words
　home. Cf. II, ii, 110, *supra:* "I cannot *speak him home*," and III, iii, 1: "charge him
　home."
67 *faint puling*] weak whining.

VOLS.   Nicanor? no.

ROM.   The same, sir.

VOLS.   You had more beard when I last saw you; but your favour
is well appeared by your tongue. What's the news in Rome?
I have a note from the Volscian state, to find you out there: 10
you have well saved me a day's journey.

ROM.   There hath been in Rome strange insurrections; the people against the senators, patricians and nobles.

VOLS.   Hath been! is it ended then? Our state thinks not so: they
are in a most warlike preparation, and hope to come upon
them in the heat of their division.

ROM.   The main blaze of it is past, but a small thing would make
it flame again: for the nobles receive so to heart the banishment of that worthy Coriolanus, that they are in a ripe aptness to take all power from the people, and to pluck from   20
them their tribunes for ever. This lies glowing, I can tell you,
and is almost mature for the violent breaking out.

VOLS.   Coriolanus banished!

ROM.   Banished, sir.

VOLS.   You will be welcome with this intelligence, Nicanor.

ROM.   The day serves well for them now. I have heard it said, the
fittest time to corrupt a man's wife is when she's fallen out
with her husband. Your noble Tullus Aufidius will appear
well in these wars, his great opposer, Coriolanus, being now
in no request of his country.   30

VOLS.   He cannot choose. I am most fortunate, thus acciden-
tally to encounter you: you have ended my business, and I
will merrily accompany you home.

ROM.   I shall, between this and supper, tell you most strange
things from Rome; all tending to the good of their adver-
saries. Have you an army ready, say you?

8–9 *your favour . . . tongue*] your identity is quite recognisable in your speech. "Favour"
means "face" or "personal appearance." "Appeared" has the significance of "made
clear or obvious." Cf. *Cymb.*, III, iv, 144: "to *appear* itself," and *Meas. for Meas.*, II,
iv, 29–30: "where their untaught love Must needs *appear* (i.e., bring to light) offence." *Appeared* is the Folio reading, for which other words including *affeer'd* (i.e.,
confirmed) and *approved* have been substituted by the editors. But no change seems
essential.

19–20 *ripe aptness*] eager readiness.

21 *This lies glowing*] The situation is compared to glowing embers about to burst into
flame.

26 *The day . . . now*] The turn of events well serves the purpose of the Volscians now.

VOLS.   A most royal one; the centurions and their charges, dis-
    tinctly billeted, already in the entertainment, and to be on
    foot at an hour's warning.
ROM.   I am joyful to hear of their readiness, and am the man, I   40
    think, that shall set them in present action. So, sir, heartily
    well met, and most glad of your company.
VOLS.   You take my part from me, sir; I have the most cause to
    be glad of yours.
ROM.   Well, let us go together.   [*Exeunt.*

SCENE IV. *Antium. Before Aufidius's House.*

Enter CORIOLANUS *in mean apparel, disguised and muffled*

COR.   A goodly city is this Antium. City,
    'T is I that made thy widows: many an heir
    Of these fair edifices 'fore my wars
    Have I heard groan and drop: then know me not;
    Lest that thy wives with spits, and boys with stones,
    In puny battle slay me.

Enter a Citizen

              Save you, sir.
CIT.   And you.
COR.   Direct me, if it be your will,
    Where great Aufidius lies: is he in Antium?   10
CIT.   He is, and feasts the nobles of the state
    At his house this night.
COR.   Which is his house, beseech you?
CIT.   This, here, before you.
COR.   Thank you, sir: farewell.
              [*Exit* Citizen.
    O world, thy slippery turns! Friends now fast sworn,
    Whose double bosoms seem to wear one heart,
    Whose hours, whose bed, whose meal and exercise
    Are still together, who twin, as 't were, in love

37 A *most royal one*] A first-rate one.
37 *centurions*] captains of a troop of a hundred men.
38 *in the entertainment*] in receipt of pay, on full allowance. Cf. "*All's Well*, IV, i, 14–15: "some band of strangers i' th' adversary's *entertainment*."

10 *lies*] lives, resides.
19 *who twin . . . in love*] who love one another like twins. Cf. *Othello*, II, iii, 204: "Though he had *twinn'd* with me."

Unseparable, shall within this hour,   20
On a dissension of a doit, break out
To bitterest enmity: so, fellest foes,
Whose passions and whose plots have broke their sleep
To take the one the other, by some chance,
Some trick not worth an egg, shall grow dear friends
And interjoin their issues. So with me:
My birth-place hate I, and my love's upon
This enemy town. I'll enter: if he slay me,
He does fair justice; if he give me way,
I'll do his country service.   [*Exit.*   30

SCENE V. *The Same. A Hall in Aufidius's House.*

Music within. Enter a Servingman

FIRST SERV.   Wine, wine, wine!—What service is here!
    I think our fellows are asleep.   [*Exit.*

Enter another Servingman

SEC. SERV.   Where's Cotus? my master calls for him. Cotus!
                                                 [*Exit.*

Enter CORIOLANUS

COR.   A goodly house: the feast smells well; but I
    Appear not like a guest.

Re-enter the first Servingman

FIRST SERV.   What would you have, friend? whence are you?
    Here's no place for you: pray, go to the door.   [*Exit.*
COR.   I have deserved no better entertainment,
    In being Coriolanus.

Re-enter second Servingman

SEC. SERV.   Whence are you, sir? Has the porter his eyes in his   10

---

21 *a dissension of a doit*] a quarrel over a farthing.
25 *Some trick*] Some toy or trifle. Cf. *T. of Shrew*, IV, iii, 67: "A knack, a toy, *a trick*, a
    baby's cap."
26 *interjoin their issues*] make their children intermarry.
27 *hate I*] Capell's correction of the Folio reading *have I*.

head, that he gives entrance to such companions? Pray, get
you out.

COR.　Away!

SEC. SERV.　"Away!" get you away.

COR.　Now thou 'rt troublesome.

SEC. SERV.　Are you so brave? I'll have you talked with anon.

Enter a third Servingman. *The first meets him*

THIRD SERV.　What fellow 's this?

FIRST SERV.　A strange one as ever I looked on: I cannot get him
out o' the house: prithee, call my master to him.　　[*Retires.*

THIRD SERV.　What have you to do here, fellow? Pray you, avoid　20
the house.

COR.　Let me but stand; I will not hurt your hearth.

THIRD SERV.　What are you?

COR.　A gentleman.

THIRD SERV.　A marvellous poor one.

COR.　True, so I am.

THIRD SERV.　Pray you, poor gentleman, take up some other station; here 's no place for you; pray you, avoid: come.

COR.　Follow your function, go, and batten on cold bits.
　　　　　　　　　　　　　　　[*Pushes him away from him.*

THIRD SERV.　What, you will not? Prithee, tell my master what a　30
strange guest he has here.

SEC. SERV.　And I shall.　　　　　　　　　　　[*Exit.*

THIRD SERV.　Where dwell'st thou?

COR.　Under the canopy.

THIRD SERV.　Under the canopy!

COR.　Ay.

THIRD SERV.　Where 's that?

COR.　I' the city of kites and crows.

THIRD SERV.　I' the city of kites and crows! What an ass it is!
Then thou dwell'st with daws too?　　　　　　　　40

COR.　No, I serve not thy master.

THIRD SERV.　How, sir! do you meddle with my master?

COR.　Ay; 't is an honester service than to meddle with thy
mistress:

---

11 *companions*] fellows. Cf. V, ii, 62, *infra*.

20–21 *avoid the house*] clear out of the house. So line 28, *infra*.

29 *batten on cold bits*] feast or gorge on cold leavings, scraps of cold dishes.

34 *the canopy*] *sc.* of heaven, the sky. Cf. *Hamlet*, II, ii, 298: "this most excellent *canopy*,
　the air."

40 *daws*] jackdaws, in the sense of simpletons, fools.

Thou pratest, and pratest; serve with thy trencher, hence!
                    [*Beats him away. Exit third* Servingman.

Enter AUFIDIUS *with the second* Servingman

AUF.   Where is this fellow?
SEC. SERV.   Here, sir: I'ld have beaten him like a dog, but for dis-
    turbing the lords within.   [*Retires.*
AUF.   Whence comest thou? what wouldst thou? thy name?
    Why speak'st not? speak, man: what's thy name?   50
COR. [*Unmuffling*]   If, Tullus,
    Not yet thou knowest me, and, seeing me, dost not
    Think me for the man I am, necessity
    Commands me name myself.
AUF.   What is thy name?
COR.   A name unmusical to the Volscians' ears,
    And harsh in sound to thine.
AUF.   Say, what 's thy name?
    Thou hast a grim appearance, and thy face
    Bears a command in 't; though thy tackle's torn,   60
    Thou show'st a noble vessel: what's thy name?
COR.   Prepare thy brow to frown:—know'st thou me yet?
AUF.   I know thee not:—thy name?
COR.   My name is Caius Marcius, who hath done
    To thee particularly, and to all the Volsces,
    Great hurt and mischief; thereto witness may
    My surname Coriolanus: the painful service,
    The extreme dangers, and the drops of blood
    Shed for my thankless country, are requited
    But with that surname; a good memory,   70
    And witness of the malice and displeasure
    Which thou shouldst bear me: only that name remains:
    The cruelty and envy of the people,
    Permitted by our dastard nobles, who
    Have all forsook me, hath devour'd the rest;
    And suffer'd me by the voice of slaves to be

---

45 *trencher*] wooden platter, on which food was cut up for eating purposes.
59–60 *thy face . . . command in 't*] Cf. North's *Plutarch*: "Yet there appeared a certain
    majesty in his countenance."
64–100 *My name is . . . service*] This speech is adapted with great literalness from
    North's *Plutarch*.
70 *a good memory*] a good memorial. Cf. V, i, 19, and V, vi, 181, *infra.* The expression
    is North's.

Hoop'd out of Rome. Now, this extremity
Hath brought me to thy hearth: not out of hope—
Mistake me not—to save my life, for if
I had fear'd death, of all the men i' the world   80
I would have 'voided thee; but in mere spite,
To be full quit of those my banishers,
Stand I before thee here. Then if thou hast
A heart of wreak in thee, that wilt revenge
Thine own particular wrongs, and stop those maims
Of shame seen through thy country, speed thee straight,
And make my misery serve thy turn: so use it
That my revengeful services may prove
As benefits to thee; for I will fight
Against my canker'd country with the spleen   90
Of all the under fiends. But if so be
Thou darest not this and that to prove more fortunes
Thou'rt tired, then, in a word, I also am
Longer to live most weary, and present
My throat to thee and to thy ancient malice;
Which not to cut would show thee but a fool,
Since I have ever follow'd thee with hate,
Drawn tuns of blood out of thy country's breast,
And cannot live but to thy shame, unless
It be to do thee service.   100

AUF.   O Marcius, Marcius!
Each word thou hast spoke hath weeded from my heart
A root of ancient envy. If Jupiter
Should from yond cloud speak divine things,
And say "'T is true," I 'ld not believe them more
Than thee, all noble Marcius. Let me twine
Mine arms about that body, where against
My grained ash an hundred times hath broke,

---

77 *Hoop'd*] Hooted. Cf. IV, vi, 154, infra: "hoot him out of the city." Thus the Folios.
  Hanmer gives the more modern spelling Whoop'd.
82 *To be full quit of*] To be entirely quits with, to pay out to the full.
84 *A heart of wreak*] A heart seeking revenge. North's expression is "if thou hast any
  heart to be wrecked (*i.e.*, wreaked, avenged) of the injuries thy enemies have done
  thee."
85–86 *maims Of shame*] shameful injuries, the spoliation of thy territory.
90 *canker'd*] malignant.
91 *the under fiends*] the fiends of hell below the earth.
108 *My grained ash*] My stout ashen spear. "Grained," which has no very definite significance as applied to the grain of wood, means here "unbroken," "strong."

And scarr'd the moon with splinters: here I clip
The anvil of my sword, and do contest   110
As hotly and as nobly with thy love
As ever in ambitious strength I did
Contend against thy valour. Know thou first,
I loved the maid I married; never man
Sigh'd truer breath; but that I see thee here,
Thou noble thing! more dances my rapt heart
Than when I first my wedded mistress saw
Bestride my threshold. Why, thou Mars! I tell thee,
We have a power on foot; and I had purpose
Once more to hew thy target from thy brawn,   120
Or lose mine arm for 't: thou hast beat me out
Twelve several times, and I have nightly since
Dreamt of encounters 'twixt thyself and me;
We have been down together in my sleep,
Unbuckling helms, fisting each other's throat;
And waked half dead with nothing. Worthy Marcius,
Had we no quarrel else to Rome but that
Thou art thence banish'd, we would muster all
From twelve to seventy, and pouring war
Into the bowels of ungrateful Rome,   130
Like a bold flood o'er-beat. O, come, go in,
And take our friendly senators by the hands,
Who now are here, taking their leaves of me,
Who am prepared against your territories,
Though not for Rome itself.
COR.   You bless me, gods!
AUF.   Therefore, most absolute sir, if thou wilt have
The leading of thine own revenges, take
The one half of my commission, and set down—
As best thou art experienced, since thou know'st   140

---

109 *scarr'd the moon with splinters*] Cf. for the hyperbolical figure *Wint. Tale*, III, iii, 89–90: "the ship *boring the moon* with her mainmast."

109–110 *I clip . . . sword*] I embrace the object which I have struck with my sword with the strength of a smith striking an anvil.

119 *a power on foot*] an army in the field.

120 *thy target from thy brawn*] thy shield from thy brawny arm.

121 *out*] outright, thoroughly.

125 *helms*] helmets.

131 *o'er-beat*] beat down, overwhelm. Thus the Folios. The word is rare. Rowe like most editors reads *o'er-bear*, *i.e.*, overflow, with which cf. IV, vi, 99: "[they] have already *O'erborne* (*i.e.*, overflowed) their way."

137 *absolute*] excellent, perfect. Cf. *Ant. and Cleop.*, I, ii, 2: "most *absolute* Alexas."

Thy country's strength and weakness—thine own ways;
Whether to knock against the gates of Rome,
Or rudely visit them in parts remote,
To fright them, ere destroy. But come in:
Let me commend thee first to those that shall
Say yea to thy desires. A thousand welcomes!
And more a friend than e'er an enemy;
Yet, Marcius, that was much. Your hand: most welcome!

> [*Exeunt* CORIOLANUS *and* AUFIDIUS.
> *The two* Servingmen *come forward.*

FIRST SERV.   Here 's a strange alteration!

SEC. SERV.   By my hand, I had thought to have strucken him   150
with a cudgel; and yet my mind gave me his clothes made a
false report of him.

FIRST SERV.   What an arm he has! he turned me about with his
finger and his thumb, as one would set up a top.

SEC. SERV.   Nay, I knew by his face that there was something in
him: he had, sir, a kind of face, methought,—I cannot tell
how to term it.

FIRST SERV.   He had so; looking as it were—Would I were
hanged, but I thought there was more in him than I could
think.   160

SEC. SERV.   So did I, I'll be sworn: he is simply the rarest man i'
the world.

FIRST SERV.   I think he is: but a greater soldier than he, you wot
one.

SEC. SERV.   Who? my master?

FIRST SERV.   Nay, it 's no matter for that.

SEC. SERV.   Worth six on him.

FIRST SERV.   Nay, not so neither: but I take him to be the greater
soldier.

SEC. SERV.   Faith, look you, one cannot tell how to say that: for   170
the defence of a town, our general is excellent.

FIRST SERV.   Ay, and for an assault too.

Re-enter third Servingman

---

151 *my mind gave me*] my mind suggested, hinted to me. The same expression appears
   in *Hen. VIII*, V, iii, 109.
154 *set up*] set spinning.
163–164 *you wot one*] you know the man I mean. Thus the Folios. For *one* many editors substitute *on* ("you wot on" being often used colloquially for "you take my
   hint"). But no change is necessary here.

THIRD SERV.   O slaves, I can tell you news; news, you rascals!
FIRST AND SEC. SERV.   What, what, what? let's partake.
THIRD SERV.   I would not be a Roman, of all nations; I had as
    lieve be a condemned man.
FIRST AND SEC. SERV.   Wherefore? wherefore?
THIRD SERV.   Why, here 's he that was wont to thwack our gen-
    eral, Caius Marcius.
FIRST SERV.   Why do you say, thwack our general?   180
THIRD SERV.   I do not say, thwack our general; but he was always
    good enough for him.
SEC. SERV.   Come, we are fellows and friends: he was ever too
    hard for him; I have heard him say so himself.
FIRST SERV.   He was too hard for him directly, to say the troth on
    't: before Corioli he scotched him and notched him like a
    carbonado.
SEC. SERV.   An he had been cannibally given, he might have
    broiled and eaten him too.
FIRST SERV.   But, more of thy news?   190
THIRD SERV.   Why, he is so made on here within as if he were
    son and heir to Mars; set at upper end o' the table; no ques-
    tion asked him by any of the senators, but they stand bald be-
    fore him. Our general himself makes a mistress of him; sanc-
    tifies himself with 's hand, and turns up the white o' the eye
    to his discourse. But the bottom of the news is, our general
    is cut i' the middle, and but one half of what he was yester-
    day; for the other has half, by the entreaty and grant of the
    whole table. He'll go, he says, and sowl the porter of Rome

183 *fellows*] companions, fellow-servants.
185 *directly*] possibly "in straightforward encounter," "hand to hand." The word is else-
    where used in the sense of "immediately" (cf. I, vi, 72, *supra*), and also in that of
    "manifestly," "obviously." Cf. *Othello*, II, i, 216: "Desdemona is *directly* in love with
    him."
186–187 *he scotched . . . like a carbonado*] hacked and cut about like a piece of meat
    slashed for broiling.
189 *broiled*] Pope's correction of the obvious Folio misreading *boyld*.
191 *so made on*] made so much of.
193 *bald*] bareheaded.
194–195 *sanctifies . . . hand*] touches his hand as if it were a holy relic. The reference
    is probably to the religious ceremony of touching a sanctified relic. Cf. *As you like
    it*, III, iv, 12–13: "his kissing is as full of sanctity as the touch of holy bread."
196 *bottom*] base, essential part.
198 *by the entreaty . . . whole table*] at the request and with the consent of all the com-
    pany.
199 *sowl*] seize or drag. The word is still common in provincial use.

gates by the ears: he will mow all down before him, and   200
leave his passage poll'd.

SEC. SERV.   And he's as like to do 't as any man I can imagine.

THIRD SERV.   Do 't! he will do 't; for, look you, sir, he has as
many friends as enemies; which friends, sir, as it were, durst
not, look you, sir, show themselves, as we term it, his friends
whilst he 's in directitude.

FIRST SERV.   Directitude! what 's that?

THIRD SERV.   But when they shall see, sir, his crest up again and
the man in blood, they will out of their burrows, like conies
after rain, and revel all with him.   210

FIRST SERV.   But when goes this forward?

THIRD SERV.   To-morrow; to-day; presently: you shall have the
drum struck up this afternoon: 't is, as it were, a parcel of
their feast, and to be executed ere they wipe their lips.

SEC. SERV.   Why, then we shall have a stirring world again. This
peace is nothing, but to rust iron, increase tailors, and breed
ballad-makers.

FIRST SERV.   Let me have war, say I; it exceeds peace as far as
day does night; it 's spritely, waking, audible, and full of vent.
Peace is a very apoplexy, lethargy, mull'd, deaf, sleepy, in-   220
sensible; a getter of more bastard children than war 's a de-
stroyer of men.

SEC. SERV.   'T is so: and as war, in some sort, may be said to be
a ravisher, so it cannot be denied but peace is a great maker
of cuckolds.

FIRST SERV.   Ay, and it makes men hate one another.

THIRD SERV.   Reason; because they then less need one another.
The wars for my money. I hope to see Romans as cheap as
Volscians. They are rising, they are rising.

FIRST AND SEC. SERV.   In, in, in, in!   [*Exeunt.*   230

---

201 *poll'd*] sheared or stripped bare (by means of plundering raids).

206 *directitude*] a blundering malapropism for "discredit." Malone substituted *discredi-
tude.*

209 *in blood*] in fighting condition.

213 *a parcel*] a part.

219 *spritely, waking*] Pope's correction of the Folio *sprightly walking* (*i.e.,* quick moving,
marching in lively fashion).

219 *full of vent*] full of go, of stir, of energy. This, and the other epithets of the sentence,
are the antitheses of the epithets "mull'd, deaf, sleepy, insensible" of the next sentence.

220 *mull'd*] flat, insipid; like wine spoilt by being boiled or over-sweetened.

228 *for my money*] for my part; a vulgar colloquialism still in use. *Englishmen for My
Money* was the name of a play by William Haughton, 1616.

SCENE VI. *Rome. A Public Place.*

Enter the two Tribunes, SICINIUS *and* BRUTUS

SIC.   We hear not of him, neither need we fear him;
     His remedies are tame i' the present peace
     And quietness of the people, which before
     Were in wild hurry. Here do we make his friends
     Blush that the world goes well; who rather had,
     Though they themselves did suffer by 't, behold
     Dissentious numbers pestering streets than see
     Our tradesmen singing in their shops and going
     About their functions friendly.
BRU.   We stood to 't in good time.   10

Enter MENENIUS

                         Is this Menenius?
SIC.   'T is he, 't is he: O, he is grown most kind
     Of late. Hail, sir!
MEN.   Hail to you both!
SIC.   Your Coriolanus is not much miss'd,
     But with his friends: the commonwealth doth stand;
     And so would do, were he more angry at it.
MEN.   All's well; and might have been much better, if
     He could have temporized.
SIC.   Where is he, hear you?   20
MEN.   Nay, I hear nothing: his mother and his wife
     Hear nothing from him.

Enter three or four Citizens

CITIZENS.   The gods preserve you both!
SIC.   God-den, our neighbours.
BRU.   God-den to you all, god-den to you all.
FIRST CIT.   Ourselves, our wives, and children, on our knees,
     Are bound to pray for you both.
SIC.   Live, and thrive!
BRU.   Farewell, kind neighbours: we wish'd Coriolanus
     Had loved you as we did.   30
CITIZENS.   Now the gods keep you!
BOTH TRI.   Farewell, farewell.   [*Exeunt* Citizens.

---

2 *His remedies . . . peace*] His means of redressing his wrongs are ineffectual in a time
  of peace like this. The Folios omit the preposition *i'*, which Theobald supplied.
4 *hurry*] commotion.

SIC.   This is a happier and more comely time
    Than when these fellows ran about the streets,
    Crying confusion.
BRU.   Caius Marcius was
    A worthy officer i' the war, but insolent,
    O'ercome with pride, ambitious past all thinking,
    Self-loving,—
SIC.   And affecting one sole throne,   40
    Without assistance.
MEN.   I think not so.
SIC.   We should by this, to all our lamentation,
    If he had gone forth consul, found it so.
BRU.   The gods have well prevented it, and Rome
    Sits safe and still without him.

Enter an Ædile

ÆD.   Worthy tribunes,
    There is a slave, whom we have put in prison,
    Reports, the Volsces with two several powers
    Are enter'd in the Roman territories,   50
    And with the deepest malice of the war
    Destroy what lies before 'em.
MEN.   'T is Aufidius,
    Who, hearing of our Marcius' banishment,
    Thrusts forth his horns again into the world;
    Which were inshell'd when Marcius stood for Rome,
    And durst not once peep out.
SIC.   Come, what talk you
    Of Marcius?
BRU.   Go see this rumourer whipp'd. It cannot be   60
    The Volsces dare break with us.
MEN.   Cannot be!
    We have record that very well it can,
    And three examples of the like have been
    Within my age. But reason with the fellow,
    Before you punish him, where he heard this,
    Lest you shall chance to whip your information,
    And beat the messenger who bids beware
    Of what is to be dreaded.

40 *affecting*] aiming at, longing for.
49 *powers*] forces, armies.
55 *his horns*] The figure is from a snail.
56 *for Rome*] in defence of Rome.
65 *reason with*] converse with.

SIC.   Tell not me: 70
  I know this cannot be.
BRU.   Not possible.

Enter a Messenger

MESS.   The nobles in great earnestness are going
  All to the senate-house: some news is come
  That turns their countenances.
SIC.   'T is this slave;
  Go whip him 'fore the people's eyes: his raising;
  Nothing but his report.
MESS.   Yes, worthy, sir,
  The slave's report is seconded; and more,   80
  More fearful, is deliver'd.
SIC.   What more fearful?
MESS.   It is spoke freely out of many mouths—
  How probable I do not know—that Marcius,
  Join'd with Aufidius, leads a power 'gainst Rome,
  And vows revenge as spacious as between
  The young'st and oldest thing.
SIC.   This is most likely!
BRU.   Raised only, that the weaker sort may wish
  Good Marcius home again.   90
SIC.   The very trick on 't.
MEN.   This is unlikely:
  He and Aufidius can no more atone
  Than violentest contrariety.

Enter a second Messenger

SEC. MESS.   You are sent for to the senate:
  A fearful army, led by Caius Marcius
  Associated with Aufidius, rages
  Upon our territories; and have already
  O'erborne their way, consumed with fire, and took
  What lay before them.   100

Enter COMINIUS

COM.   O, you have made good work!

73 *earnestness*] seriousness, anxiety.
75 *turns*] turns sour or pale.
86–87 *as spacious . . . oldest thing*] so spacious or comprehensive as to involve every-
    body, from the youngest to the oldest.
93 *atone*] be at one, be reconciled.
99 *O'erborne their way*] Overflowed their boundaries.

MEN.   What news? what news?
COM.   You have holp to ravish your own daughters, and
        To melt the city leads upon your pates;
        To see your wives dishonour'd to your noses,—
MEN.   What 's the news? what 's the news?
COM.   Your temples burned in their cement, and
        Your franchises, whereon you stood, confined
        Into an auger's bore.
MEN.   Pray now, your news?—   110
        You have made fair work, I fear me.—Pray, your news?—
        If Marcius should be join'd with Volscians,—
COM.   If!
        He is their god: he leads them like a thing
        Made by some other deity than nature,
        That shapes man better; and they follow him,
        Against us brats, with no less confidence
        Than boys pursuing summer butterflies,
        Or butchers killing flies.
MEN.   You have made good work,   120
        You and your apron-men; you that stood so much
        Upon the voice of occupation and
        The breath of garlic-eaters!
COM.   He'll shake your Rome about your ears.
MEN.   As Hercules
        Did shake down mellow fruit. You have made fair work!
BRU.   But is this true, sir?
COM.   Ay; and you 'll look pale
        Before you find it other. All the regions
        Do smilingly revolt; and who resist   130
        Are mock'd for valiant ignorance,

---

104 *leads*] sc. of the roofs, leaden coverings of the roofs.
107 *in their cement*] into their cement, till the fire crumbles even the cement between
    the stones.
108–109 *Your franchises . . . bore*] Your rights, on which you plumed yourselves, reduced
    to the narrowest compass. The bore or hole made by an auger was minute.
117 *brats*] weaklings, feeble as children.
121 *your apron-men*] your mechanics.
122 *the voice of occupation*] the approval or votes of the working class.
123 *garlic-eaters*] a common phrase of contempt for the lowest orders, with their offen-
    sively smelling breath.
125 *As Hercules . . . mellow fruit*] A farcical allusion to the story of one of Hercules'
    twelve labours which required him to gather golden apples from the garden of the
    Hesperides.
130 *smilingly*] complaisantly.

And perish constant fools. Who is 't can blame him?
Your enemies and his find something in him.
MEN.   We are all undone, unless
The noble man have mercy.
COM.   Who shall ask it?
The tribunes cannot do 't for shame; the people
Deserve such pity of him as the wolf
Does of the shepherds: for his best friends, if they
Should say "Be good to Rome," they charged him even   140
As those should do that had deserved his hate,
And therein show'd like enemies.
MEN.   'T is true:
If he were putting to my house the brand
That should consume it, I have not the face
To say "Beseech you, cease." You have made fair hands,
You and your crafts! you have crafted fair!
COM.   You have brought
A trembling upon Rome, such as was never
So incapable of help.   150
BOTH TRI.   Say not, we brought it.
MEN.   How! was it we? we loved him; but, like beasts
And cowardly nobles, gave way unto your clusters,
Who did hoot him out o' the city.
COM.   But I fear
They'll roar him in again. Tullus Aufidius,
The second name of men, obeys his points
As if he were his officer: desperation
Is all the policy, strength and defence,
That Rome can make against them.   160

Enter a troop of Citizens

MEN.   Here come the clusters.
And is Aufidius with him? You are they
That made the air unwholesome, when you cast
Your stinking greasy caps in hooting at
Coriolanus' exile. Now he 's coming;
And not a hair upon a soldier's head

132 *perish constant fools*] perish as obstinate men foolishly braving impossibilities.
140–142 *they charged . . . like enemies*] The main verbs ("charged" and "show'd") are
  here in the conditional mood. The sentence means that they would urge on him
  a charge or injunction, like men who had deserved his hatred, and they would as-
  sume the outward guise of enemies.
146 *fair hands*] a pretty piece of handiwork.
157 *his points*] his points of command, his commands.

Which will not prove a whip: as many coxcombs
As you threw caps up will he tumble down,
And pay you for your voices. 'T is no matter;
If he could burn us all into one coal,   170
We have deserved it.
CITIZENS.   Faith, we hear fearful news.
FIRST CIT.   For mine own part,
When I said, banish him, I said, 't was pity.
SEC. CIT.   And so did I.
THIRD CIT.   And so did I; and, to say the truth, so did very many
of us: that we did, we did for the best; and though we will-
ingly consented to his banishment, yet it was against our
will.
COM.   Ye 're goodly things, you voices!   180
MEN.   You have made
Good work, you and your cry! Shall 's to the Capitol?
COM.   O, ay, what else?
                              [Exeunt COMINIUS *and* MENENIUS.
SIC.   Go, masters, get you home; be not dismay'd.
These are a side that would be glad to have
This true which they so seem to fear. Go home,
And show no sign of fear.
FIRST CIT.   The gods be good to us! Come, masters, let 's home.
I ever said we were i' the wrong when we banished him.
SEC. CIT.   So did we all. But, come, let's home.   190
                              [Exeunt Citizens.
BRU.   I do not like this news.
SIC.   Nor I.
BRU.   Let 's to the Capitol: would half my wealth
Would buy this for a lie!
SIC.   Pray, let us go.   *[Exeunt.*

SCENE VII. *A Camp at a small distance from Rome.*

Enter AUFIDIUS *with his* Lieutenant

AUF.   Do they still fly to the Roman?
LIEU.   I do not know what witchcraft 's in him, but
Your soldiers use him as the grace 'fore meat,
Their talk at table and their thanks at end;

182 *cry*] pack.

And you are darken'd in this action, sir,
Even by your own.
AUF.   I cannot help it now,
Unless, by using means, I lame the foot
Of our design. He bears himself more proudlier,
Even to my person, than I thought he would   10
When first I did embrace him: yet his nature
In that's no changeling; and I must excuse
What cannot be amended.
LIEU.   Yet I wish, sir—
I mean for your particular—you had not
Join'd in commission with him; but either
Had borne the action of yourself, or else
To him had left it solely.
AUF.   I understand thee well; and be thou sure,
When he shall come to his account, he knows not   20
What I can urge against him. Although it seems,
And so he thinks, and is no less apparent
To the vulgar eye, that he bears all things fairly,
And shows good husbandry for the Volscian state,
Fights dragon-like, and does achieve as soon
As draw his sword, yet he hath left undone
That which shall break his neck or hazard mine,
Whene'er we come to our account.
LIEU.   Sir, I beseech you, think you he'll carry Rome?
AUF.   All places yield to him ere he sits down;   30
And the nobility of Rome are his:
The senators and patricians love him too:
The tribunes are no soldiers; and their people
Will be as rash in the repeal, as hasty
To expel him thence. I think he'll be to Rome
As is the osprey to the fish, who takes it
By sovereignty of nature. First he was
A noble servant to them; but he could not
Carry his honours even: whether 't was pride,
Which out of daily fortune ever taints   40

5 *darken'd*] thrown into the shade.
15 *for your particular*] in your own personal interest.
24 *shows good husbandry*] shows good management.
26–28 *yet he hath left . . . our account*] These lines clearly mean that Coriolanus' omission of some unspecified act is certain to imperil his own life and that of Aufidius.
29 *carry*] conquer, take.
36–37 *As is the osprey . . . nature*] Fish are said to make no sort of resistance to the attack of the osprey but turn on their backs and surrender to the bird without a struggle.

The happy man; whether defect of judgement,
To fail in the disposing of those chances
Which he was lord of; or whether nature,
Not to be other than one thing, not moving
From the casque to the cushion, but commanding peace
Even with the same austerity and garb
As he controll'd the war; but one of these—
As he hath spices of them all, not all,
For I dare so far free him—made him fear'd,
So hated, and so banish'd: but he has a merit,   50
To choke it in the utterance. So our virtues
Lie in the interpretation of the time;
And power, unto itself most commendable,
Hath not a tomb so evident as a chair
To extol what it hath done.
One fire drives out one fire; one nail, one nail;
Rights by rights fouler, strengths by strengths do fail.
Come, let 's away. When, Caius, Rome is thine,
Thou art poor'st of all; then shortly art thou mine.

                                    [*Exeunt.*

41 *happy*] prosperous, fortunate.
43–45 *nature . . . cushion*] a stubborn uniformity of nature which could not fittingly
     make the transition from the soldier's helmet to the civil magistrate's armchair.
47 *controll'd the war*] exercised control in war-time.
48 *spices of them all*] Aufidius credits Coriolanus with some taste of the three several
     vices which he has imputed to him, *viz.*, the pride that comes of success, inability to
     make good use of the fruits of victory, and lack of power to accommodate his habit
     of military command to the exercise of civil authority.
50–51 *he has a merit . . . utterance*] his merit is such as ought to choke the utterance of
     censure.
51–52 *So our virtues . . . the time*] So our virtues depend for their estimation on the way
     in which they are adapted to the circumstances of the time.
53–55 *And power . . . it hath done*] The general meaning of these difficult lines is: And
     power, though meritoriously earned and rightly generating self-satisfaction, is liable
     to no graver ruin than what comes of self-laudation.
57 *Rights by rights fouler . . . fail*] The construction is very obscure and irregular. As it
     stands, the line means that just rights or titles fail in the presence of rights or titles
     which are of worse validity, and strengths of one kind succumb to strengths of an-
     other. It would, however, seem reasonable here to regard *fouler* as a misprint, and to
     accept Dyce's happy emendation of *falter*.

ACT V.

SCENE I. *Rome. A Public Place.*

Enter MENENIUS, COMINIUS, SICINIUS *and* BRUTUS, *the two*
    Tribunes, *with others*

MENENIUS.   No, I'll not go: you hear what he hath said
    Which was sometime his general, who loved him
    In a most dear particular. He call'd me father:
    But what o' that? Go, you that banish'd him;
    A mile before his tent fall down, and knee
    The way into his mercy: nay, if he coy'd
    To hear Cominius speak, I'll keep at home.
COM.   He would not seem to know me.
MEN.   Do you hear?
COM.   Yet one time he did call me by my name: 10
    I urged our old acquaintance, and the drops
    That we have bled together. Coriolanus
    He would not answer to: forbad all names;
    He was a kind of nothing, titleless,
    Till he had forged himself a name o' the fire
    Of burning Rome.
MEN.   Why, so: you have made good work!
    A pair of tribunes that have rack'd fair Rome,
    To make coals cheap: a noble memory!

2 *Which*] Who; the antecedent is "he," *i.e.*, Cominius (line 1).
 3 *In a most dear particular*] In a most affectionate and private intimacy.
 6–7 *coy'd To hear*] was coy of hearing, was reluctant to hear.
13 *forbad all names*] declined to respond to any name.
15 *o' the fire*] out of the fire.
18 *rack'd fair Rome*] striven for, strained every nerve for, Rome. Cf. *Merch. of Ven.*, I, i,
    181: "(My credit) . . . shall be *rack'd*, even to the uttermost." Thus Pope. The Folios
    read *wrack'd for Rome* which Dyce changed, quite needlessly, into *wreck'd fair Rome*.
19 *To make coals cheap*] With the result of cheapening fuel by making Rome itself ma-
    terial for fire.
19 *memory*] memorial. Cf. IV, v, 70, *supra*.

COM.   I minded him how royal 't was to pardon   20
  When it was less expected: he replied,
  It was a bare petition of a state
  To one whom they had punish'd.
MEN.   Very well:
  Could he say less?
COM.   I offer'd to awaken his regard
  For 's private friends: his answer to me was,
  He could not stay to pick them in a pile
  Of noisome musty chaff: he said, 't was folly,
  For one poor grain or two, to leave unburnt,   30
  And still to nose the offence.
MEN.   For one poor grain or two!
  I am one of those; his mother, wife, his child,
  And this brave fellow too, we are the grains:
  You are the musty chaff, and you are smelt
  Above the moon: we must be burnt for you.
SIC. Nay, pray, be patient: if you refuse your aid
  In this so never-needed help, yet do not
  Upbraid's with our distress. But sure, if you
  Would be your country's pleader, your good tongue,   40
  More than the instant army we can make,
  Might stop our countryman.
MEN.   No, I 'll not meddle.
SIC.   Pray you, go to him.
MEN.   What should I do?
BRU.   Only make trial what your love can do
  for Rome, towards Marcius.
MEN.   Well, and say that Marcius
  Return me, as Cominius is return'd,
  Unheard; what then?   50
  But as a discontented friend, grief-shot
  With his unkindness? say 't be so?
SIC.   Yet your good will

---

22 *a bare petition*] a threadbare request, a petition of no substance.
28 *in a pile*] from, or out of, a heap.
31 *nose the offence*] suffer the annoyance, endure the disagreeable odour of the unde-
 stroyed offensive matter.
36 *Above the moon*] Skyhigh.
41 *the instant army we can make*] the army we can raise on the instant.
47 *towards Marcius*] in regard to Coriolanus.
51 *grief-shot*] grief-stricken.

    Must have that thanks from Rome, after the measure
    As you intended well.
MEN.   I 'll undertake 't:
    I think he 'll hear me. Yet, to bite his lip
    And hum at good Cominius, much unhearts me.
    He was not taken well; he had not dined:
    The veins unfill'd, our blood is cold, and then   60
    We pout upon the morning, are unapt
    To give or to forgive; but when we have stuff'd
    These pipes and these conveyances of our blood
    With wine and feeding, we have suppler souls
    Than in our priest-like fasts: therefore I'll watch him
    Till he be dieted to my request,
    And then I'll set upon him.
BRU.   You know the very road into his kindness,
    And cannot lose your way.
MEN.   Good faith, I'll prove him,   70
    Speed how it will. I shall ere long have knowledge
    Of my success.   [*Exit.*
COM.   He 'll never hear him.
SIC.   Not?
COM.   I tell you, he does sit in gold, his eye
    Red as 't would burn Rome; and his injury
    The gaoler to his pity. I kneel'd before him;
    'T was very faintly he said "Rise;" dismiss'd me
    Thus, with his speechless hand: what he would do,
    He sent in writing after me; what he would not,   80
    Bound with an oath to yield to his conditions:

---

54 *after the measure . . . well*] in proportion to the goodness of your intention.
58 *hum*] mutter without speaking a word. Cf. *Macb.*, III, vi, 41–42: "The cloudy mes-
    senger turns he his back, And *hums.*"
59 *taken well*] approached at a favourable moment.
61 *We pout upon the morning*] We are surly and sullen in the early morning.
66 *dieted to my request*] well fed so as to be in a humour to grant my request.
70 *prove*] make proof or trial of.
72 *my success*] the result of my effort.
75 *sit in gold*] sit enthroned in imperial splendour.
76–77 *his injury . . . pity*] the feeling of the wrong done him restrained his pity, kept it
    under lock and key.
80–81 *what he would not . . . conditions*] The construction is difficult. These words with
    this punctuation must summarise the effect of the message which Coriolanus sent
    in writing after Cominius. He announced in effect that he would do nothing, he
    would not make reasonable terms, being bound by oath to make his fellow-country-
    men yield to his harsh conditions.

So that all hope is vain,
Unless his noble mother, and his wife;
Who, as I hear, mean to solicit him
For mercy to his country. Therefore, let 's hence,
And with our fair entreaties haste them on.   [*Exeunt.*

SCENE II. *Entrance to the Volscian Camp before Rome.*
Two Sentinels on Guard.

Enter to them, MENENIUS

FIRST SEN.   Stay: whence are you?
SEC. SEN.   Stand, and go back.
MEN.   You guard like men; 't is well: but, by your leave,
    I am an officer of state, and come
    To speak with Coriolanus.
FIRST SEN.   From whence?
MEN.   From Rome.
FIRST SEN.   You may not pass, you must return: our general
    Will no more hear from thence.
SEC. SEN.   You 'll see your Rome embraced with fire, before   10
    You 'll speak with Coriolanus.
MEN.   Good my friends,
    If you have heard your general talk of Rome,
    And of his friends there, it is lots to blanks
    My name hath touch'd your ears: it is Menenius.
FIRST SEN.   Be it so; go back: the virtue of your name
    Is not here passable.
MEN.   I tell thee, fellow,
    Thy general is my lover: I have been
    The book of his good acts, whence men have read   20
    His fame unparallel'd haply amplified;
    For I have ever verified my friends,

83 *Unless his noble mother*] Unless (there be hope in) his noble mother.

14 *lots to blanks*] any number of prizes to any number of blanks. Cf. *Rich. III*, I, ii, 237: "all the world to nothing."

19 *lover*] dear friend; a common usage. Cf. *Jul. Cæs.*, III, ii, 13: "Romans, countrymen, and *lovers.*"

20 *The book*] The recorder or reporter.

22 *verified*] supported by true testimony, spoken the truth of. The word is not known elsewhere in this sense, and *glorified* and *magnified* have been suggested in its place.

Of whom he 's chief, with all the size that verity
Would without lapsing suffer: nay, sometimes,
Like to a bowl upon a subtle ground,
I have tumbled past the throw, and in his praise
Have almost stamp'd the leasing: therefore, fellow,
I must have leave to pass.

FIRST SEN.   Faith, sir, if you had told as many lies in his behalf
as you have uttered words in your own, you should not pass   30
here; no, though it were as virtuous to lie as to live chastely.
Therefore go back.

MEN.   Prithee, fellow, remember my name is Menenius, always
factionary on the party of your general.

SEC. SEN.   Howsoever you have been his liar, as you say you
have, I am one that, telling true under him, must say, you
cannot pass. Therefore go back.

MEN.   Has he dined, canst thou tell? for I would not speak with
him till after dinner.

FIRST SEN.   You are a Roman, are you?   40

MEN.   I am, as thy general is.

FIRST SEN.   Then you should hate Rome, as he does. Can you,
when you have pushed out your gates the very defender of
them, and, in a violent popular ignorance, given your
enemy your shield, think to front his revenges with the easy
groans of old women, the virginal palms of your daughters,
or with the palsied intercession of such a decayed dotant as
you seem to be? Can you think to blow out the intended fire
your city is ready to flame in, with such weak breath as this?
No, you are deceived; therefore, back to Rome, and prepare   50
for your execution: you are condemned; our general has
sworn you out of reprieve and pardon.

MEN.   Sirrah, if thy captain knew I were here, he would use me
with estimation.

25–27 *upon a subtle ground . . . leasing*] upon a deceptive bowling green, I have gone
beyond the mark, and in my praise of him almost given the stamp of my authority
to lying. "Leasing" is an archaic word for "lie" or "lying." Cf. *Psalms*, iv, 2: "How
long will ye . . . seek after *leasing*?" and *Tw. Night*, I, v, 91.

34 *factionary*] busy, active.

45 *front his revenges*] meet, resist his vengeance.

45 *easy*] easily uttered, and therefore unworthy of notice.

46 *virginal palms*] innocent hands raised in supplication. Cf. *2 Hen. VI*, V, ii, 52: "tears
virginal."

47 *dotant*] dotard.

54 *estimation*] respect.

FIRST SEN.   Come, my captain knows you not.

MEN.   I mean, thy general.

FIRST SEN.   My general cares not for you. Back, I say, go; lest I
let forth your half-pint of blood;—back,—that 's the utmost
of your having:—back.

MEN.   Nay, but, fellow, fellow—   60

Enter CORIOLANUS *and* AUFIDIUS

COR.   What 's the matter?

MEN.   Now, you companion, I'll say an errand for you: you shall
know now that I am in estimation; you shall perceive that a
Jack guardant cannot office me from my son Coriolanus:
guess, but by my entertainment with him, if thou standest
not i' the state of hanging, or of some death more long in
spectatorship and crueller in suffering; behold now
presently, and swoon for what's to come upon thee. The glorious gods sit in hourly synod about thy particular prosperity,
and love thee no worse than thy old father Menenius does!   70
O my son, my son! thou art preparing fire for us; look thee,
here's water to quench it. I was hardly moved to come to
thee; but being assured none but myself could move thee, I
have been blown out of your gates with sighs; and conjure
thee to pardon Rome and thy petitionary countrymen. The
good gods assuage thy wrath, and turn the dregs of it upon
this varlet here,—this, who, like a block, hath denied my ac-
cess to thee.

COR.   Away!

MEN.   How! away!   80

COR.   Wife, mother, child, I know not. My affairs

58–59 *the utmost of your having*] the utmost you will get.

62 *companion*] fellow. Cf. IV, v, 11, *supra.*

62 *I'll say an errand for you*] I'll make a report of you, deliver a message in your behalf;
in other words, I'll tell of your behaviour to me.

64 *a Jack guardant cannot office me*] a Jack on guard cannot keep me by his officious-
ness. "A Jack guardant" is almost equivalent to "a Jack in office." "Office" as a verb
is rare.

65 *but by*] *by* is Malone's insertion in the Folio text.

67 *in spectatorship*] in the act of beholding, from the sightseer's point of view.

68–69 *The glorious gods . . . synod*] Cf. *Pericles*, I, i, 10: "The senate house of planets all
did sit." Menenius is here addressing Coriolanus.

74 *your gates*] the gates of your city Rome. For *your gates*, the reading of the first three
Folios, the Fourth Folio reasonably substitutes *our gates*.

Are servanted to others: though I owe
My revenge properly, my remission lies
In Volscian breasts. That we have been familiar,
Ingrate forgetfulness shall poison rather
Than pity note how much. Therefore be gone.
Mine ears against your suits are stronger than
Your gates against my force. Yet, for I loved thee,
Take this along; I writ it for thy sake,
And would have sent it. [*Gives him a letter.*] Another word,
    Menenius,   90
I will not hear thee speak. This man, Aufidius,
Was my beloved in Rome: yet thou behold'st.
AUF.   You keep a constant temper.
                    [*Exeunt* CORIOLANUS *and* AUFIDIUS.
FIRST SEN.   Now, sir, is your name Menenius?
SEC. SEN.   'T is a spell, you see, of much power: you know the
    way home again.
FIRST SEN.   Do you hear how we are shent for keeping your
    greatness back?
SEC. SEN.   What cause, do you think, I have to swoon?
MEN.   I neither care for the world nor your general: for such   100
    things as you, I can scarce think there's any, ye're so slight.
    He that hath a will to die by himself fears it not from an-
    other: let your general do his worst. For you, be that you are,
    long; and your misery increase with your age! I say to you, as
    I was said to, Away!   [*Exit.*
FIRST SEN.   A noble fellow, I warrant him.
SEC. SEN.   The worthy fellow is our general: he's the rock, the
    oak not to be wind-shaken.   [*Exeunt.*

---

81 *Are servanted to*] Are made servants to, serve.
81–83 *though I owe . . . breasts*] though my revenge is my personal right, the power of
    pardon (is no affair of mine, but) is the business of the Volscians.
85–86 *Ingrate forgetfulness . . . how much*] The forgetfulness of ingratitude shall kill as
    by poison rather than that pity should give any sign of what the amount of our in-
    timacy was.
93 *a constant temper*] a temper of firm faith to your new friends.
97 *shent*] shamed, rebuked; an archaic word.
102 *die by himself*] die by his own hand.

SCENE III. *The Tent of Coriolanus.*

Enter CORIOLANUS, AUFIDIUS, *and others*

COR.   We will before the walls of Rome to-morrow
    Set down our host. My partner in this action,
    You must report to the Volscian lords how plainly
    I have borne this business.
AUF.   Only their ends
    You have respected; stopp'd your ears against
    The general suit of Rome; never admitted
    A private whisper, no, not with such friends
    That thought them sure of you.
COR.   This last old man,   10
    Whom with a crack'd heart I have sent to Rome,
    Loved me above the measure of a father,
    Nay, godded me indeed. Their latest refuge
    Was to send him; for whose old love I have,
    Though I show'd sourly to him, once more offer'd
    The first conditions, which they did refuse
    And cannot now accept; to grace him only
    That thought he could do more, a very little
    I have yielded to: fresh embassies and suits,
    Nor from the state nor private friends, hereafter   20
    Will I lend ear to. [*Shout within.*] Ha! what shout is this?
    Shall I be tempted to infringe my vow
    In the same time 't is made? I will not.

Enter, in mourning habits, VIRGILIA, VOLUMNIA, *leading young*
    MARCIUS, VALERIA, *and* Attendants.

    My wife comes foremost; then the honour'd mould
    Wherein this trunk was framed, and in her hand
    The grandchild to her blood. But out, affection!
    All bond and privilege of nature, break!
    Let it be virtuous to be obstinate.
    What is that curtsy worth? or those doves' eyes,
    Which can make gods forsworn? I melt, and am not   30
    Of stronger earth than others. My mother bows;
    As if Olympus to a molehill should
    In supplication nod; and my young boy
    Hath an aspect of intercession, which

3 *plainly*] honestly, without subterfuge.
16 *The first conditions*] Cf. V, i, 81, *supra*, and note.

    Great nature cries "Deny not." Let the Volsces
    Plough Rome, and harrow Italy: I 'll never
    Be such a gosling to obey instinct; but stand,
    As if a man were author of himself
    And knew no other kin.
VIR.   My lord and husband!   40
COR.   These eyes are not the same I wore in Rome.
VIR.   The sorrow that delivers us thus changed
    Makes you think so.
COR.   Like a dull actor now
    I have forgot my part and I am out,
    Even to a full disgrace. Best of my flesh,
    Forgive my tyranny; but do not say,
    For that "Forgive our Romans." O, a kiss
    Long as my exile, sweet as my revenge!
    Now, by the jealous queen of heaven, that kiss   50
    I carried from thee, dear, and my true lip
    Hath virgin'd it e'er since. You gods! I prate,
    And the most noble mother of the world
    Leave unsaluted: sink, my knee, i' the earth;   [*Kneels.*
    Of thy deep duty more impression show
    Than that of common sons.
VOL.   O, stand up blest!
    Whilst, with no softer cushion than the flint,
    I kneel before thee, and unproperly
    Show duty, as mistaken all this while   60
    Between the child and parent.   [*Kneels.*
COR.   What is this?
    Your knees to me? to your corrected son?
    Then let the pebbles on the hungry beach

41–43 *These eyes . . . think so*] Coriolanus means that his disposition is changed, that he
    looks on things differently. Virgilia interprets his use of the word "eyes" quite liter-
    ally, and explains his imagined failure of eyesight to the change wrought in the ap-
    pearance and dress of herself and her companions.
45–46 *I am out . . . disgrace*] I have broken down to my complete disgrace. Cf. *Sonnet*
    xxiii, i, 2: "As an unperfect actor . . . is put besides his part." For this use of "out," cf.
    L. L. L., V, ii, 172: "They do not mark me and that brings me *out*."
50 *the jealous queen of heaven*] Juno whom the Romans regarded as the goddess of mar-
    riage and the avenger of connubial infidelity. Cf. Pericles, II, iii, 30: "By Juno that is
    queen of marriage."
52 *I prate*] Theobald's correction of the Folio reading *I pray*.
64 *hungry*] sterile, barren; as in "*hungry* soil." There is no need to give the word the
    meaning of "cruel," "hungry for shipwrecks." The insignificance and worthlessness
    of the pebbles is the essential point.

Fillip the stars; then let the mutinous winds
Strike the proud cedars 'gainst the fiery sun,
Murdering impossibility, to make
What cannot be, slight work.

VOL.   Thou art my warrior;
I holp to frame thee. Do you know this lady?   70

COR.   The noble sister of Publicola,
The moon of Rome; chaste as the icicle
That 's curdied by the frost from purest snow
And hangs on Dian's temple: dear Valeria!

VOL.   This is a poor epitome of yours,
Which by the interpretation of full time
May show like all yourself.

COR.   The god of soldiers,
With the consent of supreme Jove, inform
Thy thoughts with nobleness, that thou mayst prove   80
To shame unvulnerable, and stick i' the wars
Like a great sea-mark, standing every flaw
And saving those that eye thee!

VOL.   Your knee, sirrah.

COR.   That 's my brave boy!

VOL.   Even he, your wife, this lady and myself
Are suitors to you.

COR.   I beseech you, peace:
Or, if you 'ld ask, remember this before:
The thing I have forsworn to grant may never   90
Be held by you denials. Do not bid me

65 *Fillip the stars*] Smite the stars. The figure is of the worthless pebbles violently lifted
to the height of the stars.

67 *Murdering impossibility*] Annihilating impossibility, making everything possible.

70 *holp*] the archaic form of "helped." Cf. V, vi, 41, *infra.*

71 *The noble sister of Publicola*] Plutarch describes Valeria, sister of an eminent Roman
general, M. Valerius Publius (surnamed Publicola), as "greatly honoured and rever-
enced among all the Romans." According to Plutarch, she suggested the present dep-
utation.

72 *The moon of Rome*] Diana, the goddess of chastity, was also goddess of the moon.

73 *curdied*] congealed. Thus the Folios. Rowe substituted *curdled*, which may be right.

75 *This is a poor epitome . . . yourself*] This is a miniature copy of you which in the full
development of time may present a complete image of yourself. Volumnia is, of
course, speaking of her little grandson.

81 *stick*] remain steadfast.

82 *a great sea-mark, standing every flaw*] a beacon at sea, resisting every squall.

90–91 *The thing . . . denials*] You must not reckon me to deny to you personally the
thing my oath forbids me granting anybody.

91 *denials*] Thus the first three Folios. The Fourth reads more reasonably *denial.* Capell
retained *denials,* but substituted *things* for *thing* in line 90.

　　　Dismiss my soldiers, or capitulate
　　　Again with Rome's mechanics: tell me not
　　　Wherein I seem unnatural: desire not
　　　To allay my rages and revenges with
　　　Your colder reasons.
Vol.　　　　　　　　　O, no more, no more!
　　　You have said you will not grant us any thing;
　　　For we have nothing else to ask, but that
　　　Which you deny already: yet we will ask;　　　　　　　100
　　　That, if you fail in our request, the blame
　　　May hang upon your hardness: therefore hear us.
Cor.　　Aufidius, and you Volsces, mark; for we'll
　　　Hear nought from Rome in private. Your request?
Vol.　　Should we be silent and not speak, our raiment
　　　And state of bodies would bewray what life
　　　We have led since thy exile. Think with thyself
　　　How more unfortunate than all living women
　　　Are we come hither: since that thy sight, which should
　　　Make our eyes flow with joy, hearts dance with comforts,　　　110
　　　Constrains them weep and shake with fear and sorrow;
　　　Making the mother, wife and child, to see
　　　The son, the husband and the father, tearing
　　　His country's bowels out. And to poor we
　　　Thine enmity's most capital: thou barr'st us
　　　Our prayers to the gods, which is a comfort
　　　That all but we enjoy; for how can we,
　　　Alas, how can we for our country pray,
　　　Whereto we are bound, together with thy victory,
　　　Whereto we are bound? alack, or we must lose　　　　　120
　　　The country, our dear nurse, or else thy person,
　　　Our comfort in the country. We must find
　　　An evident calamity, though we had
　　　Our wish, which side should win; for either thou
　　　Must, as a foreign recreant, be led

　92 *capitulate*] come to terms, negotiate.
　95 *allay*] moderate, mitigate. Cf. II, i, 42, *supra:* "*allaying* Tiber."
101 *fail in*] fail to grant.
102 *hardness*] harshness, obduracy.
105–204 *Should we be silent . . . mortal to him*] The whole of this passage closely fol-
　　　lows, though with some dramatic modification and amplification, the words of
　　　North's *Plutarch*.
106 *bewray*] betray, display.
111 *Constrains . . . shake*] Constrains the eye to weep and the heart to shake.
125 *recreant*] traitor.

With manacles thorough our streets, or else
Triumphantly tread on thy country's ruin,
And bear the palm for having bravely shed
Thy wife and children's blood. For myself, son,
I purpose not to wait on fortune till   130
These wars determine: if I cannot persuade thee
Rather to show a noble grace to both parts
Than seek the end of one, thou shalt no sooner
March to assault thy country than to tread—
Trust to 't, thou shalt not—on thy mother's womb,
That brought thee to this world.

VIR.   Ay, and mine,
That brought you forth this boy, to keep your name
Living to time.

BOY.   A' shall not tread on me;   140
I'll run away till I am bigger, but then I'll fight.

COR.   Not of a woman's tenderness to be,
Requires nor child nor woman's face to see.
I have sat too long.   [*Rising.*

VOL.   Nay, go not from us thus.
If it were so that our request did tend
To save the Romans, thereby to destroy
The Volsces whom you serve, you might condemn us,
As poisonous of your honour: no; our suit
Is, that you reconcile them: while the Volsces   150
May say "This mercy we have show'd," the Romans,
"This we received;" and each in either side
Give the all-hail to thee, and cry "Be blest
For making up this peace!" Thou know'st, great son,
The end of war's uncertain, but this certain,
That if thou conquer Rome, the benefit
Which thou shalt thereby reap is such a name
Whose repetition will be dogg'd with curses;
Whose chronicle thus writ: "The man was noble,
But with his last attempt he wiped it out,   160

---

126 *thorough*] Johnson's awkward change, for the sake of the metre, of the Folio reading *through*. It is better to retain *through* and leave the line short of a foot, pronouncing "manacles" as a dissyllable and pausing before "or."
131 *determine*] end, conclude.
132 *both parts*] both parties, both sides.
153 *the all-hail*] the full note of greeting.
160 *with his last attempt . . . out*] with his last enterprise he cancelled his noble reputation.

Destroy'd his country, and his name remains
To the ensuing age abhorr'd." Speak to me, son:
Thou hast affected the fine strains of honour,
To imitate the graces of the gods;
To tear with thunder the wide cheeks o' the air,
And yet to charge thy sulphur with a bolt
That should but rive an oak. Why dost not speak?
Think'st thou it honourable for a noble man
Still to remember wrongs? Daughter, speak you:
He cares not for your weeping. Speak thou, boy: 170
Perhaps thy childishness will move him more
Than can our reasons. There's no man in the world
More bound to 's mother, yet here he lets me prate
Like one i' the stocks. Thou hast never in thy life
Show'd thy dear mother any courtesy;
When she, poor hen, fond of no second brood,
Has cluck'd thee to the wars, and safely home,
Loaden with honours. Say my request 's unjust,
And spurn me back: but if it be not so,
Thou art not honest, and the gods will plague thee,   180
That thou restrain'st from me the duty which
To a mother's part belongs. He turns away:
Down, ladies; let us shame him with our knees.
To his surname Coriolanus 'longs more pride
Than pity to our prayers. Down: an end;
This is the last: so we will home to Rome,
And die among our neighbours. Nay, behold 's:
This boy, that cannot tell what he would have,
But kneels and holds up hands for fellowship,
Does reason our petition with more strength   190
Than thou hast to deny 't. Come, let us go:
This fellow had a Volscian to his mother;
His wife is in Corioli, and his child
Like him by chance. Yet give us our dispatch:

---

163 *the fine strains*] the refined and generous impulses. Cf. *Troil. and Cress.*, II, ii, 154:
    "so degenerate a *strain* as this."
166 *charge thy sulphur*] charge thy lightning (which preceded and was thought to pro-
    pel the thunderbolt).
174 *Like one i' the stocks*] Like one in some ignominious position.
190–191 *Does reason . . . to deny 't*] There is more force of reason in the boy's support
    of our petition than in your resolve to refuse it.
193–194 *his child Like him by chance*] his child resembles him by accident, is not really
    his son.

       I am hush'd until our city be a-fire,
       And then I'll speak a little.
COR. [*After holding her by the hand, silent*]   O mother, mother!
       What have you done? Behold, the heavens do ope,
       The gods look down, and this unnatural scene
       They laugh at. O my mother, mother! O!   200
       You have won a happy victory to Rome;
       But, for your son, believe it, O, believe it,
       Most dangerously you have with him prevail'd,
       If not most mortal to him. But let it come.
       Aufidius, though I cannot make true wars,
       I 'll frame convenient peace. Now, good Aufidius,
       Were you in my stead, would you have heard
       A mother less? or granted less, Aufidius?
AUF.   I was moved withal.
COR.   I dare be sworn you were: 210
       And, sir, it is no little thing to make
       Mine eyes to sweat compassion. But, good sir,
       What peace you'll make, advise me: for my part,
       I 'll not to Rome, I 'll back with you; and pray you,
       Stand to me in this cause, O mother! wife!
AUF. [*Aside*]   I am glad thou hast set thy mercy and thy honour
       At difference in thee: out of that I'll work
       Myself a former fortune.
                 [*The* Ladies *make signs to* CORIOLANUS.
COR. [*To* VOLUMNIA, VIRGILIA, *&c.*] Ay, by and by:—
       But we will drink together; and you shall bear   220
       A better witness back than words, which we
       On like conditions will have counter-seal'd.
       Come, enter with us. Ladies, you deserve
       To have a temple built you: all the swords
       In Italy, and her confederate arms,
       Could not have made this peace.   [*Exeunt.*

215 *Stand to me in this cause*] Support me in this business.
217–218 *I'll work . . . fortune*] I will take advantage of this course of events to regain my
    former position of independence.
220 *we will drink together*] Apparently Coriolanus proposes to drink the healths of
    Aufidius and the Volscian leaders.
223–224 *Ladies . . . built you*] According to Plutarch, a temple to Fortune was built by
    order of the Senate in honour of these ladies' intercession. The edifice was built at
    their own expense; for they refused the offer of the Senate to bear the cost.

SCENE IV. *Rome. A Public Place.*

Enter MENENIUS *and* SICINIUS

MEN.   See you yond coign o' the Capitol, yond corner-stone?
SIC.   Why, what of that?
MEN.   If it be possible for you to displace it with your little finger, there is some hope the ladies of Rome, especially his
mother, may prevail with him. But I say there is no hope in
't: our throats are sentenced, and stay upon execution.
SIC.   Is 't possible that so short a time can alter the condition of
a man?
MEN.   There is differency between a grub and a butterfly; yet
your butterfly was a grub. This Marcius is grown from man   10
to dragon: he has wings; he 's more than a creeping thing.
SIC.   He loved his mother dearly.
MEN.   So did he me: and he no more remembers his mother
now than an eight-year-old horse. The tartness of his face
sours ripe grapes: when he walks, he moves like an engine,
and the ground shrinks before his treading: he is able to
pierce a corselet with his eye; talks like a knell, and his hum
is a battery. He sits in his state, as a thing made for
Alexander. What he bids be done, is finished with his bidding. He wants nothing of a god but eternity and a heaven to   20
throne in.
SIC.   Yes, mercy, if you report him truly.
MEN.   I paint him in the character. Mark what mercy his
mother shall bring from him: there is no more mercy in him
than there is milk in a male tiger; that shall our poor city
find: and all this is long of you.
SIC.   The gods be good unto us!
MEN.   No, in such a case the gods will not be good unto us.
When we banished him, we respected not them; and, he re-
turning to break our necks, they respect not us.   30

---

6 *stay upon execution*] only wait for execution.
7 *condition*] disposition.
9 *differency*] Thus the First Folio. The later Folios have the ordinary form *difference*.
14 *an eight-year-old horse*] sc. remembers his dam.
15 *an engine*] sc. of war, a battering-ram.
18 *state*] chair of state. Cf. V, i, 75, *supra*: "he does sit in gold."
18–19 *as a thing made for Alexander*] like a thing intended to represent Alexander the
    Great, like a statue of Alexander.
23 *in the character*] in the true character.
26 *long of you*] along of you, owing to you.

Enter a Messenger

MESS.   Sir, if you 'ld save your life, fly to your house:
      The plebeians have got your fellow-tribune,
      And hale him up and down, all swearing, if
      The Roman ladies bring not comfort home,
      They'll give him death by inches.

Enter another Messenger

SIC.   What's the news?
SEC. MESS.   Good news, good news; the ladies have prevail'd,
      The Volscians are dislodged, and Marcius gone:
      A merrier day did never yet greet Rome,
      No, not the expulsion of the Tarquins.   40
SIC.   Friend,
      Art thou certain this is true? is it most certain?
SEC. MESS.   As certain as I know the sun is fire:
      Where have you lurk'd, that you make doubt of it?
      Ne'er through an arch so hurried the blown tide,
      As the recomforted through the gates. Why, hark you!
               [*Trumpets; hautboys; drums beat; all together.*
      The trumpets, sackbuts, psalteries and fifes,
      Tabors and cymbals and the shouting Romans,
      Make the sun dance. Hark you!   [*A shout within.*
MEN.   This is good news: 50
      I will go meet the ladies. This Volumnia
      Is worth of consuls, senators, patricians,
      A city full; of tribunes, such as you,
      A sea and land full. You have pray'd well to-day:
      This morning for ten thousand of your throats
      I 'ld not have given a doit. Hark, how they joy!
               [*Music still, with shouts.*
SIC.   First, the gods bless you for your tidings; next,
      Accept my thankfulness.
SEC. MESS.   Sir, we have all
      Great cause to give great thanks.   60
SIC.   They are near the city?

45–46 *Ne'er through . . . the gates*] Doubtless a reference to the noisy rush of water
    through the arches of London bridge. Cf. *Lucrece*, 1667–1668: "As through an arch
    the violent roaring tide Outruns the eye that doth behold his haste."
49 *Make the sun dance*] The sun was believed to dance on Easter day. Cf. Suckling's
    Ballad on a Wedding, verse 8: "But oh! she *dances* such a way, No *sun upon an Easter
    day* Is half so fine a sight."

SEC. MESS.   Almost at point to enter.
SIC.   We will meet them,
    And help the joy.   [Exeunt.

SCENE V. *The Same. A Street near the Gate.*

Enter two Senators *with* VOLUMNIA, VIRGILIA, VALERIA, &c. *pass-
    ing over the stage, followed by* Patricians *and others*

FIRST SEN.   Behold our patroness, the life of Rome!
    Call all your tribes together, praise the gods,
    And make triumphant fires; strew flowers before them:
    Unshout the noise that banish'd Marcius,
    Repeal him with the welcome of his mother;
    Cry "Welcome, ladies, welcome!"
ALL.   Welcome, ladies,
    Welcome!   [*A flourish with drums and triumpets. Exeunt.*

SCENE VI. *Corioli. A Public Place.*

Enter TULLUS AUFIDIUS, *with* Attendants

AUF.   Go tell the lords o' the city I am here:
    Deliver them this paper: having read it,
    Bid them repair to the market-place, where I,
    Even in theirs and in the commons' ears,
    Will vouch the truth of it. Him I accuse
    The city ports by this hath enter'd, and
    Intends to appear before the people, hoping
    To purge himself with words: dispatch.
                                     [*Exeunt* Attendants.

Enter three or four Conspirators *of* AUFIDIUS' *faction*

    Most welcome!
FIRST CON.   How is it with our general?   10
AUF.   Even so
    As with a man by his own alms empoison'd,
    And with his charity slain.

---

62 *at point to enter*] on the point of entering.

SCENE V] Dyce first noted the beginning of a new short scene here.
  6 *ports*] gates; so I, vii, 1, *supra.*

Sec. Con.   Most noble sir,
  If you do hold the same intent wherein
  You wish'd us parties, we 'll deliver you
  Of your great danger.
Auf.   Sir, I cannot tell:
  We must proceed as we do find the people.
Third Con.   The people will remain uncertain whilst   20
  'Twixt you there's difference; but the fall of either
  Makes the survivor heir of all.
Auf.   I know it,
  And my pretext to strike at him admits
  A good construction. I raised him, and I pawn'd
  Mine honour for his truth: who being so heighten'd,
  He water'd his new plants with dews of flattery,
  Seducing so my friends; and, to this end,
  He bow'd his nature, never known before
  But to be rough, unswayable and free.   30
Third Con.   Sir, his stoutness
  When he did stand for consul, which he lost
  By lack of stooping, —
Auf.   That I would have spoke of:
  Being banish'd for 't, he came unto my hearth;
  Presented to my knife his throat: I took him,
  Made him joint-servant with me, gave him way
  In all his own desires, nay, let him choose
  Out of my files, his projects to accomplish,
  My best and freshest men, served his designments   40
  In mine own person, holp to reap the fame
  Which he did end all his; and took some pride
  To do myself this wrong: till at the last

15–16 *If you do hold . . . parties*] If you hold to the purpose (of killing Coriolanus) in
   which you desired our co-operation.
25 *A good construction*] A plausible explanation.
27 *He water'd . . . flattery*] He cherished his new allies by plentifully flattering them. Mr.
   Craig quotes North's translation of Plutarch's Life of Cato (ed. 1595, p. 373): "he
   could make men *water their plants* (*i.e.*, behave submissively) that heard him."
29 *bow'd*] bent, adapted.
30 *free*] outspoken.
39 *my files*] my musters.
40 *served his designments . . . person*] helped his plans with my personal service.
41 *holp*] the archaic form of "helped." Cf. V, iii, 70, *supra*.
42 *Which he did end all his*] The whole of which he garnered or stored for himself.
   "End" is still common in dialect as a verb meaning "to get in," or "store," crops.
   Shakespeare also uses in the same sense the verb "in," of which "end" is really only
   a dialectic variation. Cf. *All's Well*, I, iii, 43: "to *in* the crop."

    I seem'd his follower, not partner, and
    He waged me with his countenance, as if
    I had been mercenary.
FIRST CON.   So he did, my lord:
    The army marvell'd at it, and in the last,
    When he had carried Rome and that we look'd
    For no less spoil than glory—   50
AUF.   There was it:
    For which my sinews shall be stretch'd upon him.
    At a few drops of women's rheum, which are
    As cheap as lies, he sold the blood and labour
    Of our great action: therefore shall he die,
    And I'll renew me in his fall. But hark!
    [*Drums and trumpets sound, with great shouts of the people.*
FIRST CON.   Your native town you enter'd like a post,
    And had no welcomes home; but he returns,
    Splitting the air with noise.
SEC. CON.   And patient fools,   60
    Whose children he hath slain, their base throats tear
    With giving him glory.
THIRD CON.   Therefore, at your vantage,
    Ere he express himself, or move the people
    With what he would say, let him feel your sword,
    Which we will second. When he lies along,
    After your way his tale pronounced shall bury
    His reasons with his body.
AUF.   Say no more:
    Here come the lords.   70

Enter the Lords *of the city*

ALL THE LORDS.   You are most welcome home.
AUF.   I have not deserved it.
    But, worthy lords, have you with heed perused
    What I have written to you?
LORDS.   We have.
FIRST LORD.   And grieve to hear 't.

45 *He waged me . . . mercenary*] He paid me (like a hireling) with his patronising favour.
49 *carried*] conquered, taken.
52 *For which . . . upon him*] For which I will attack him to the full extent of my strength.
54 *As cheap as lies*] Cf. *Hamlet*, III, ii, 348: "it is easy as lying."
57 *a post*] a postboy, a messenger.
63 *at your vantage*] at an opportunity favourable to you.
67 *After your way his tale pronounced*] The tale that may be told of him narrated in your
    own words.

What faults he made before the last, I think
Might have found easy fines: but there to end
Where he was to begin, and give away
The benefit of our levies, answering us   80
With our own charge, making a treaty where
There was a yielding,—this admits no excuse.

AUF.   He approaches: you shall hear him.

Enter CORIOLANUS, *marching with drum and colours; the
commoners being with him*

COR.   Hail, lords! I am return'd your soldier;
No more infected with my country's love
Than when I parted hence, but still subsisting
Under your great command. You are to know,
That prosperously I have attempted, and
With bloody passage led your wars even to
The gates of Rome. Our spoils we have brought home   90
Do more than counterpoise a full third part
The charges of the action. We have made peace,
With no less honour to the Antiates
Than shame to the Romans: and we here deliver,
Subscribed by the consuls and patricians,
Together with the seal o' the senate, what
We have compounded on.

AUF.   Read it not, noble lords;
But tell the traitor, in the highest degree
He hath abused your powers.   100

COR.   Traitor! how now!

AUF.   Ay, traitor, Marcius!

COR.   Marcius!

AUF.   Ay, Marcius, Caius Marcius: dost thou think
I'll grace thee with that robbery, thy stol'n name
Coriolanus, in Corioli?
You lords and heads o' the state, perfidiously
He has betray'd your business, and given up,
For certain drops of salt, your city Rome,
I say "your city," to his wife and mother;   110
Breaking his oath and resolution, like

---

78 *easy fines*] easy condonation.
80–81 *answering . . . charge*] making us pay our own expenses for the war, giving us no
   return for our own money.
86 *parted*] departed.
109 *drops of salt*] tears.

    A twist of rotten silk; never admitting
    Counsel o' the war; but at his nurse's tears
    He whined and roar'd away your victory;
    That pages blush'd at him, and men of heart
    Look'd wondering each at other.
COR.   Hear'st thou, Mars?
AUF.   Name not the god, thou boy of tears!
COR.   Ha!
AUF.   No more.   120
COR.   Measureless liar, thou hast made my heart
    Too great for what contains it. "Boy!" O slave!
    Pardon me, lords, 't is the first time that ever
    I was forced to scold. Your judgements, my grave lords,
    Must give this cur the lie: and his own notion—
    Who wears my stripes impress'd upon him; that
    Must bear my beating to his grave—shall join
    To thrust the lie unto him.
FIRST LORD.   Peace, both, and hear me speak.
COR.   Cut me to pieces, Volsces; men and lads,   130
    Stain all your edges on me. "Boy!" false hound!
    If you have writ your annals true, 't is there,
    That, like an eagle in a dove-cote, I
    Flutter'd your Volscians in Corioli;
    Alone I did it. "Boy!"
AUF.   Why, noble lords,
    Will you be put in mind of his blind fortune,
    Which was your shame, by this unholy braggart,
    'Fore your own eyes and ears?
ALL CONSP.   Let him die for 't.   140
ALL THE PEOPLE.   "Tear him to pieces." "Do it presently." "He
    killed my son." "My daughter." "He killed my cousin
    Marcus." "He killed my father."
SEC. LORD.   Peace, ho! no outrage: peace!
    The man is noble, and his fame folds-in
    This orb o' the earth. His last offences to us
    Shall have judicious hearing. Stand, Aufidius,
    And trouble not the peace.
COR.   O that I had him,

112 *twist*] skein.
118 *boy of tears*] cry-baby, blubbering boy. "Boy" is a term of contempt.
125 *notion*] sense, understanding.
131 *your edges*] your sword-blades.
145 *folds-in . . . earth*] embraces, overspreads the whole world.
147 *judicious hearing*] judicial inquiry or trial.

With six Aufidiuses, or more, his tribe,   150
To use my lawful sword!
AUF.   Insolent villain!
ALL CONSP.   Kill, kill, kill, kill, kill him!
                    [*The* Conspirators *draw, and kill* CORIOLANUS:
                              AUFIDIUS *stands on his body.*
LORDS.   Hold, hold, hold, hold!
AUF.   My noble masters, hear me speak.
FIRST LORD.   O Tullus,—
SEC. LORD.   Thou hast done a deed whereat valour will weep.
THIRD LORD.   Tread not upon him. Masters all, be quiet;
Put up your swords.
AUF.   My lords, when you shall know—as in this rage   160
Provokèd by him, you cannot—the great danger
Which this man's life did owe you, you 'll rejoice
That he is thus cut off. Please it your honours
To call me to your senate, I'll deliver
Myself your loyal servant, or endure
Your heaviest censure.
FIRST LORD.   Bear from hence his body;
And mourn you for him: let him be regarded
As the most noble corse that ever herald
Did follow to his urn.   170
SEC. LORD.   His own impatience
Takes from Aufidius a great part of blame.
Let 's make the best of it.
AUF.   -   My rage is gone,
And I am struck with sorrow. Take him up:
Help, three o' the chiefest soldiers; I 'll be one.
Beat thou the drum, that it speak mournfully:
Trail your steel pikes. Though in this city he
Hath widow'd and unchilded many a one,
Which to this hour bewail the injury,   180
Yet he shall have a noble memory.
Assist.   [*Exeunt, bearing the body of* CORIOLANUS.
                              A dead march sounded.

162 *did owe you*] made you liable to, exposed you to.
169–170 *As the noble corse . . . to his urn*] Shakespeare associates with Roman funeral
     customs the prominent share taken in the funeral ceremonies of great persons in
     his own day by the professional herald who pronounced the formal title of the de-
     ceased when the coffin was laid in the grave.
171 *His own impatience*] Coriolanus' irascibility.
178 *Trail your steel pikes*] Soldiers at funerals dragged their pikes along the ground when
     attending the funeral of a comrade as nowadays they reverse their muskets.
181 *a noble memory*] a noble memorial.